THE VEILED HUNTRESS

CORINNE M. KNIGHT

GUANYIN
PUBLISHING

BLURB

Outside the hallowed halls of Roslyn Academy, the Order of the Dragon unscrupulously nurtures supernatural entities to further their clandestine designs.

As Jade, Ash, Alessandra, and Vlad return to the academy, their eagerly awaited reunion with Lucien is tinged with a heavy sense of longing. Avery, the woman who holds Lucien's heart captive, remains ensnared within the treacherous clutches of her malevolent father.

With an unwavering determination to bring her back, Lucien seeks the assistance of a formidable witch from beyond the academy's confines—a specialist skilled in the art of finding the lost. Guided by the faint but hopeful breadcrumbs Avery has left behind, they inch ever closer to her concealed location, racing against the relentless passage of time.

A gallant rescue team assembles, ready to face any peril in their relentless quest to liberate Avery from the abyss of darkness. Meanwhile, Avery awakens within the chilling confines of her father's lair, fully aware of the nightmarish experiments that await her. When Lucien's reassuring voice reaches her, promising salvation, it ignites a fragile spark of hope within her.

Yet, as her father's malevolent experiments intensify, Avery's resilience and determination are tested to their limits. Can she endure the ceaseless onslaught long enough for her rescuers to set her free?

Chapter 1

As acrid smoke surrounded her, Avery felt a sharp sting in her eyes, blurring her vision into a hazy mist. Amid the crackling flames, her pulse seemed to echo in her ears, a foreboding feeling weighing heavily in her stomach.

The commanding figure, whose memory had haunted Avery's restless dreams, remained seated on his ominous obsidian throne. The emotions flooded over her, especially the burning anger at how her childhood had been twisted and stolen for his benefit.

Avery felt a chilling shiver as her father's cold voice echoed in the chamber. "Welcome back, daughter," it purred, as sleek and lethal as a dagger concealed in silk.

Avery tightly clenched her hands, desperately searching for courage. "I won't be your puppet any longer," she declared, praying her voice did not tremble and betray her.

Darmon observed her, his pale eyes devoid of life just like a midwinter moon. A slow, predatory smile stretched across his face. "You can never escape your destiny. It is carved into your very bones. You will always be my aide and serve my ambitions."

Unwanted memories flooded Avery's mind; excruciating experiments that melted flesh from bone and the endless trials where a single failure meant death. The soul-crushing moments where her heart had shattered, along with her trust in her father. She shook under the immense weight of the past, wondering if she had the strength to keep its sinister grasp from stealing her future.

Avery took a steeling breath, desperately willing strength into her trembling limbs. "I decide my fate now," she asserted. "I won't let you manipulate me again."

Darmon's condescending click of the tongue struck Avery like a heart-wrenching whip, fuelling her anger and humiliation.

His icy stare sliced through her, as sharp and invasive as a blade splitting flesh from bone. She fought the urge to recoil, to shield her vulnerability from his ruthless gaze, which seemed to dissect the very secrets of her soul.

"You truly believed you could escape me, daughter?" Darmon purred, a predator toying with helpless prey. He rose from his imposing obsidian throne, darkness swirling about him like a vengeful spectre.

A hurricane of conflicted emotions thrashed inside her. Defiant anger warred with lingering grief for the loving father she had always longed for him to be. Her heart seemed on the verge of bursting from the pressure.

"It is your destiny to serve my ambitions," Darmon pronounced, his tone invoking images of unmarked graves and forgotten victims. "With your powers harnessed, we shall conquer the supernatural world and seize control of the realm."

Unwanted tears pricked hotly at Avery's eyes, but she refused to shed them, to show even that small weakness. "I won't allow you to twist me into a weapon," she insisted, nails carving crescents into her fists. "My life belongs with Lucien now."

A cruel smile split Darmon's stony face. His pale eyes stared through her, devoid of the faintest spark of empathy or mercy. "That vampire has filled your head with frivolous fantasies, but it is far too late to fight fate's design."

In a sudden burst of preternatural speed, his claws clamped her throat in an iron grip. Skin sizzled under the unnatural heat of his grasp. Agony erupted within Avery, but she clung desperately to her love for Lucien—an escape keeping her tethered as she drifted toward unrelenting darkness.

Through the bleak haze smothering her mind, she gritted out her vow. "You won't succeed..."

Oblivion slowly consumed Avery's vision. Darmon's voice rolled out like a chilling bell in the still night air. "When you wake, we will have started anew," it purred.

As darkness enveloped Avery's dwindling

consciousness, her thoughts instinctively sought Lucien with an unwavering, desperate yearning.

"Lucien... don't lose hope," she whispered weakly, clutching at the lifeline of their bond as her strength seeped away. "I will find my way back to you again."

Though the world fell away around her into endless shadow, Avery focused every ounce of her unwavering determination on their connection, mentally screaming his name.

Lucien... listen. My father is coming...

In a tranquil instant, she experienced the reassuring warmth of Lucien's presence, akin to an unseen, radiant hand softly entwining with hers. A tiny flame of faith kindled within her heart. She could almost feel the comforting pressure of Lucien clasping her hand, his voice echoing distantly but edged with worry.

Avery! What happened? Where are you?

Before she could respond, intense pain erupted through her body, originating from Darmon's ruthless efforts to sever their bond. Agony wracked through her as she involuntarily cried out. Lucien's desperate voice grew fainter as darkness dragged Avery backwards.

No! Avery, don't go! I will find you, I swear it... Just

hang on...

Avery drifted aimlessly in that vast, impenetrable night, her thoughts sluggish and disjointed. Unwanted memories assaulted her—the agony of endless experiments, being forced to betray Lucien. It would be dangerously easy to surrender hope here, to let exhaustion overpower her.

But Avery clung fiercely to one unshakeable truth: she would never again be Darmon's puppet. She was a fighter who carved her own destiny. If only she could break free of this smothering darkness, she would stand against him once more. *Wake up!* she commanded her leaden body. But she felt terrifyingly frail, drained of all power and will.

"You are mine now, daughter." Her father's bone-chilling voice echoed through her mind. "Resign yourself to your fate."

The battle within Avery still burned. "No..." she murmured, her whisper dripping with defiance. Though physically subdued, her spirit remained indomitable. Her resolve to defy him remained staunch.

She wandered through the vast emptiness, her eyes scouring for a glimmer in the engulfing shadows that menaced to swallow her essence. The conviction that guiding stars endured in this abyss held onto her, akin to Lucien's steadfast love—a constant beacon in her heart.

Avery plunged relentlessly into the void, feeling a sense of self fraying at the edges with each heart-beat. But she clung to the last burning shreds of courage, fanning their fire with memories of stolen hours with Lucien—secret meetings at the Old Church, the electric thrill of their first kiss, the rare smiles that transformed him. She wrapped these precious moments around her like shields against despair.

As endless darkness pressed down on her, smothering like a physical weight, Avery felt hope-lessness's insidious poison seeping through the cracks in her resolve. "Please," she whispered into the void, "give me a fighting chance. I cannot endure this alone."

With the last dregs of her strength, Avery hurled her plea into the lightless abyss, praying some benevolent force lingered within these shadows. "Lucien, I need you now more than ever. Please, you must find me..."

Suddenly, a vision pierced the gloom; Lucien standing defiantly before Darmon's shadowy throne, his features etched with rage.

"You will not claim her," he pronounced, his

voice heavy with power and shaking the very air. Quick as light, his Katana slashed through the clinging darkness. Blinding radiance erupted from the silver blade, banishing the oppressive shadows.

The vision vanished as suddenly as it had appeared, leaving longing and renewed belief tangled within Avery like threads pulling her in opposite directions. Had she merely conjured a fantasy from desperation? Or had Lucien truly discovered some way to bridge the unfathomable divide separating them?

She had no notion whether their bond could transcend this cursed oblivion. Still, she poured every ounce of her waning spirit into that fragile life-line of belief.

Suddenly, Avery felt a subtle shift in the darkness, followed by the faintest sliver of a beloved voice whispering her name, impossibly distant but achingly familiar.

"Avery..."

Elation surged wildly within her. "Lucien!" she cried with raw desperation, willing her voice to breach the gap. "Save me, I beg you."

Through their tenuous link, Avery felt the full force of Lucien's emotions collide into her—bottomless love entwined with rage and determination. She focused every fibre of her being on strengthening their connection, pushing against the abyss with all her might until she could feel the brush of his spirit against hers.

The shadows shuddered, seeming to recoil from the brilliance of their bond.

His voice resonated through her mind with conviction, each word a glowing promise. *"I am coming for you."*

Avery clung to the fragile spark of confidence now kindling within her. Together, their love could illuminate even the blackest night.

Chapter 2

LUCIEN PACED THE MOONLIT COURTYARD, A TEMPEST of dread and frustration churning within him. Each minute that crawled by in silence felt like another merciless cut across his already ravaged heart. The quiet itself seemed alive, a stifling veil weighing down upon him.

Sinister thoughts haunted Lucien's mind, painted in indelible shades of blood and anguish. Had Darmon already extinguished the fiery light in Avery's defiant eyes? Subjected her to unimaginable agony simply because he could? Lucien dug his nails ruthlessly into his palms until crimson welled up, channelling waves of rage at his own helplessness to protect her.

At last, his comrades shuffled into view, their hollow expressions mirroring the bleak pain roiling inside Lucien. Haunted shadows lingered in their downcast eyes, echoes of whatever fresh trauma the Order had so callously inflicted. Lucien's soul cried out in anguish at the visible evidence of their suffering. He yearned to erase the vivid pain marking their features, to restore even a glimmer of hope's light back into their weary hearts. But Lucien feared they had lost such innocence now, just one more casualty in this endless conflict shadowed by his old employer's cruelty.

As the battered group hobbled inside, Lucien's gaze raked their bodies, taking stock of each visible wound his comrades had been forced to endure. "What new torments did the Order inflict?" he bit out through clenched teeth as he gently treated a vicious gash marring Jade's arm.

She offered a faint, hollow laugh, barely disguising bone-deep exhaustion. "Nothing we have not survived before." But her flickering eyes betrayed the truth: Darmon was slowly extinguishing even their formidable endurance.

After settling the group as comfortably as their ravaged forms would allow, Lucien joined Vlad, where he broodingly watched the hearth's dying embers decay to sullen ash.

Vlad's lip curled in disgust. "We should raze the Order's strongholds for this. Make them truly suffer as we have endured." His knuckles whitened as if already wrapped around his tormentors' throats.

But Lucien just gazed sightlessly into the faint glow, all light leached from his blue eyes by fear and anguish. "More violence will only breed darker shadows. We need light." His voice dropped to a tortured whisper. "Or I fear we shall lose hers forever."

The words seemed to drain the feverish rage from Vlad. Grim understanding softened his expression. They had won the battle with Azaroth, but this larger war still threatened to snuff all fragile confidence, starting with the bright flame of Avery's spirit if they could not reach her in time...

ALESSANDRA'S CRIES, RAW WITH ANGUISH, SLICED through the stillness of the night. Her mind, ensnared in torment's unyielding grip, shivered under the onslaught of vivid nightmares. In this maelstrom of despair, Vlad's murmurs drifted like a calming balm, his words weaving a sanctuary around her. Gently, he held her quivering form, anchoring her to safety, and drawing her away from the precipice of her fears.

From the doorway, Lucien observed them, a deep ache hollowing his chest. Silently, he sent up a fervent prayer into the shadows, smothering his soul. "Avery, wherever you are, I swear I will save you." He clung to this vow like an ember kindling against despair's frigid gusts. "Our love must be the beacon to guide you home and banish the darkness haunting you..."

He started his tireless pacing in the moon-washed courtyard as if sheer momentum could somehow close the unfathomable distance still separating him from Avery. Each restless step marked his doggedness. He was determined to search through every hidden crevice of existence if it meant holding his love safely in his arms again. Until then, only love and faith could accompany him in the small hours of this interminable night.

At last, Vlad emerged, his grim features softening with empathy as he met Lucien's hollow gaze. In that shared moment bloomed an unspoken camaraderie. No matter what fresh hells awaited them on the path ahead, they would confront the flames together to shield their loved ones. Without the persistent glow of Avery and Alessandra's spirits, only a void would remain, and they were firmly committed to not letting endless darkness claim their victory.

"How's Alessandra doing?" Lucien finally whispered, loathe to further disturb the fraught stillness.

Vlad exhaled heavily. "Ill at ease still. The memory of my blood on her hands haunts her. She woke screaming, begging my forgiveness for nearly taking my life while enthralled." His tortured gaze met Lucien's. "I fear I will lose her to remorse," Vlad confessed, his voice dropping lower. Beneath the weight of Alessandra's agony, his formerly proud shoulders sagged.

Lucien gripped Vlad's arm, willing his own conviction into the gesture. "You know she was the Order's helpless puppet then. The guilt belongs to her tormentors alone."

Vlad grimaced. "I know, yet she cannot absolve herself. She flinches from my touch, fearing she will cause me harm again." Raw anguish carved new lines across his weary features.

Lucien swallowed against the ache in his own throat, grasping for words of solace. "Give her time," he urged gently. "Keep showing Alessandra that your love remains unshaken."

At last, Vlad summoned a small but grateful smile. "As ever, your counsel provides needed perspective, nephew. My bond with Alessandra will mend, I am certain, however long the process may take."

Lucien's chest constricted, the journey ahead seeming endless and shrouded in gloom. "I, too, must keep my trust in Avery," he whispered. "And hope that she can find her way back through whatever darkness imprisons her now."

Vlad's weathered features softened with solemn empathy. He cradled Lucien's cheek in one battle-scarred hand as if the gesture could help shoulder his torment.

"Have courage," the older vampire urged gently. "No force can eternally separate what destiny has firmly linked. Either we shall reclaim the women we hold dear from this darkness, or we shall spend eternity combing every obscure realm in our relentless pursuit of their light."

Their gazes locked, pouring waves of conviction and a shared purpose that words could never adequately capture.

"For now, try to rest," Vlad implored. "The nights to come will demand every ounce of resilience and valour we can muster."

Lucien shut his eyes in the face of a wave of sorrow. How did one rest when cruel oblivion threatened to consume his other half? When the soul cried out constantly for its missing piece, its vital orbit thrown disastrously off balance?

Still, he forced a brusque nod of acquiescence to Vlad's wisdom. Too many relied on him holding the fraying threads of composure and leadership together to allow himself to unravel now. Somehow, he must distil all his volcanic grief into steely, enduring patience and fortitude. Anything less could mean surrendering his guiding star—his beloved Avery—to inescapable darkness forever.

With Vlad's departure, silence once more

claimed dominion over the moonlit courtyard. Lucien resumed his ceaseless pacing, each weighted step echoing with the agonising beat of uncertainty throbbing sickeningly inside him.

Amidst the stillness surrounding him, an odd sensation sparked along the periphery of his consciousness—subtle yet oddly magnetic, like the phantom tug of a muted heartbeat straining toward connection.

Lucien froze in his tracks, every finely honed sense focusing to razor sharpness. Could it be...? Reaching desperately along the slender filament of psychic connection binding his soul to Avery's, he poured every mote of concentration and yearning into that fragile lifeline.

And then, scarcely daring to breathe in the stillness, he felt it. The faintest brush of Avery's beloved essence against his. Fragmented and impossibly distant, yet undeniably her. A maelstrom of elation and terror crashed through Lucien. She lived, struggling across some unfathomable gulf to reach him from whatever malign prison Darmon had devised.

Not wasting a heartbeat more, Lucien hurled his own devotion back to her along with their tenuous thread of connection.

"Avery! What happened? Where are you?"

Silence.

"I will find you, I swear it... Just hang on..."

The stillness absorbed his ardent vow. Somewhere, somehow, perhaps she had caught his whispered promise between one faltering breath and the next.

Drawing a shaky breath, Lucien tilted his head toward the soft moonlight above in silent supplication. *"I am coming for you."*

The connection dimmed as swiftly as a guttering candle, leaving Lucien stranded in crushing silence and doubt. Yet even that fleeting, fragile lifeline had reignited the smouldering embers of conviction buried deep within his embattled spirit.

He clung to that tenacious light desperately, letting it guide him like a lone star scintillating against the endless night. No matter how lost Avery herself seemed in some vast, dark abyss, Lucien silently vowed he would follow that flame's beckoning promise anywhere. He'd traverse straight through the darkest hellscape and guarded perils imaginable just to shelter his beloved safely in his arms once more.

With siege-hardened resolve reinforcing his every fibre, Lucien turned on his heel to abandon the empty, moon-washed courtyard, his boots echoing with fierce purpose. His thoughts galvanised now around assembling the forces and strategic counsel needed for the battle looming ominously ahead. The time they so desperately required to save Avery was swiftly bleeding away.

As he rushed to phone Lóthurr, his heart pounded with anxiety, hope, and a simmering fury barely held in check. "Have you heard anything about Avery?" he demanded urgently.

Sympathy filled Lóthurr's tone, though it carried a heavy weight of gravity. "I'm afraid Darmon has taken the girl deeper underground. But don't lose faith—help is on the way."

Lucien's grip on the phone tightened, and he willed himself to remain steady. "Who's going to help us out?"

"A gypsy witch. A valued ally and friend to our cause," Lóthurr explained. "Her magic is formidable. If your bond with Avery remains, she might be able to trace her."

Lucien closed his eyes for a moment, releasing a shaky breath. Relief washed over him like a soothing wave. "Thanks, buddy. With the witch on our side, we can get through these never-ending shadows."

"Stay strong, Lucien. We will bring her back safely," Lóthurr promised.

After ending the call, Lucien's resolve grew stronger, preparing him for the upcoming challenges. He had spent too much time hiding, watching evil grow unchecked. That was about to change. Now, with courageous friends bound together by loyalty, they were ready to fight back and restore what was right. They would either lift the darkness covering the land, or Lucien would break through it himself to save what he cherished most.

At the sound of approaching footsteps, Lucien turned sharply, a predator sensing vulnerable prey. But it was only Vlad who stepped from the gloom, face carved with solemn purpose.

"Any developments on Avery?" Lucien inquired through gritted teeth, his gaze drilling into the other man in search of any revealing information.

Vlad responded with a solemn shake of his head. "None as yet. However, there are murmurs of peculiar demonic activity near the old cathedral. It might provide a slender lead."

Lucien's fists clenched, resisting the rage surging within him. Although patience was not his strong suit, he promised himself to persevere, for Avery's sake.

Vlad placed a firm and supportive grip on his

shoulder. "Stay strong for her. We will find her and exact vengeance on those who took her."

Lucien gave a tight nod, a silent pledge to contain his burning anger until Avery was secure. Yet, if any misfortune had touched her at Darmon's hands, nothing on this earthly realm could shield him from the tempest of Lucien's impending fury.

For the love of his life, Lucien was prepared to walk the fine line between brutality and self-control. Until they were together again, the inner beast would constantly cry out for justice. She was his beacon, his essence of humanity; without her, there was nothing but a deep, dark void.

After parting ways with Vlad, Lucien secluded himself in his chamber, enduring the excruciating passage of hours until the arrival of the gypsy witch. He once again reached out along with the psychic bond shared with Avery, whispering words of solace.

Even though the connection was muted, he could sense her essence, flickering weakly like a candle bravely resisting the engulfing darkness. "Hold on, my love," he silently urged. "I'm coming for you."

THE NEXT DAY, NEWS REACHED THE ACADEMY OF THE Romani envoy nearing its gates. Lucien rushed downstairs, his caution swept away by the currents of desperate hope.

The massive doors creaked open, revealing two imposing figures adorned with their unmistakable clan tattoos. In their midst walked a petite woman, her features hidden beneath a hooded shawl.

Lucien's gaze locked onto the scene, his intensity unfaltering. "Are you here to help us?"

The female advanced, throwing back her hood to unveil her face. "I am Madame Leana of the Crescent clan," she affirmed, her voice possessing a melodic yet resolute cadence. Sharp eyes peered into Lucien's soul with a penetrating gaze.

Lucien nodded, resolution etched across his features. "Let's get started. There's a life at stake."

The witch's lips curved into a knowing smile. "Darkness will not triumph today. Shall we?"

With Madame Leana's arrival, Lucien swiftly guided her to the academy's ritual chamber. Every fibre of his being urged him to act immediately in locating Avery, yet he clung to the fragile threads of his patience.

"Before we dive in, just a heads up," Lucien warned, "Lord Darmon's no joke. He's got some serious dark magic up his sleeve. Not many have gone up against him and come back to talk about it."

Madame Leana nodded gravely. "Your apprehension is justified. But trust in this. I've harnessed magics just as ancient. The shadows will not triumph."

Her words, resounding with confidence, reignited hope within Lucien. Finally, with the witch's aid, they would have what was needed to unravel the mystery shrouding Avery's whereabouts. This was more than a mere breakthrough; it was as if a beacon had been lit in the darkest night, guiding them towards reuniting with Avery and mending the torn fabric of their fate.

In the centre of the chamber, Madame Leana gathered arcane tools of candles, crystals, and elixirs. She turned to Lucien. "Focus on your connection to the girl. I will handle the rest."

Lucien closed his eyes, immersing himself in the ethereal link that bound him to Avery. Madame

Leana's once melodious voice adopted an eerie rhythm as she commenced the ritual.

The chamber became laden with oppressive power, yet Lucien shut it all out, focusing solely on the delicate lifeline connecting their souls. *Avery... guide me to you...*

Madame Leana's voice rose, reaching a mesmerising crescendo. The flames of nearby candles seemed to stretch towards her as if drawn by the swirling energy enveloping the gypsy witch.

White-knuckled, Lucien gripped the edges of the carved table. His entire being was entrenched in the psychic tether to Avery, urging the witch's spell to penetrate the shadowy shroud that concealed her.

The chanting reached a breathtaking climax. The chamber quivered, ancient artefacts rattling on their shelves. Lucien squeezed his eyes shut against the blinding light emanating from Madame Leana's ritual tools.

When he dared to open them again, the room had stilled. Yet Madame Leana stood before him, her gaze ablaze with purpose.

"It is done," she said. "I know where the girl is being held."

A surge of relief mingled with an undercurrent

of fury within Lucien. Finally, after endless nights of waiting, he could take decisive action.

"Tell me," he commanded, his veins pulsing with bloodlust. He would tear Lord Darmon's stronghold stone from stone to reclaim Avery if need be.

Madame Leana's melodic voice echoed with gravity. "Patience, vampire. Recklessness jeopardises all. We must strategize our attack and gather allies."

Lucien, though consumed by the desire to rescue Avery, mastered his savage instincts. He knew she spoke with wisdom. The time had come for judicious action, not mindless chaos.

Chapter 3

IN THE DEPTHS OF BLACKNESS, AVERY CLUNG TO HER lifeline—the cherished memories of Lucien's love. Pain gradually pierced the void, pulling her into consciousness.

Reluctantly, she opened her eyes, though her

vision remained blurred. A hulking demon hovered over her, and a darker figure observed from the shadows. Her father.

"... admirable resilience..." the creature rumbled. "Time for another dose..."

Agony erupted through Avery's veins as the demon injected her. Straining against her bonds, her back arched.

This was his bidding, Avery realised. Yet, she would not break. Especially not when her last thoughts were of Lucien.

Despite the demon's injections causing fresh agony, Avery refused to cry out. She wouldn't give her father the satisfaction.

She comprehended his twisted purpose for this torture—he aimed to mould her into the perfect assassin for the Order. Not entirely vampire nor demon, but a hybrid amalgamation, endowed with the powers of both races.

Revulsion simmered within Avery. Her sire cared nothing for her humanity or free will; she was merely a vessel for his vile ambitions.

Even in the present moment, he watched with clinical indifference as the demon pierced her flesh repeatedly, infusing her veins with its cursed blood.

Avery could feel the foul substance seeping through her, warping her spirit.

She clenched her teeth, determined to resist and aid Lucien in thwarting her father's nefarious plans. In her mind, she repeated Lucien's name like a mantra, clinging to memories of his love to preserve her sense of self.

Her inner light dimmed, dwarfed by hellish shadows. Yet, as long as she clung to Lucien, hope endured. Each injection of demonic blood felt like liquid fire coursing through Avery's veins. Despite thrashing against her bonds until the leather cut into her skin, she couldn't escape the relentless agony.

Throughout the ordeal, her father observed dispassionately, jotting notes on a clipboard. To him, she was a mere experiment, a subject to be tested and disposed of if necessary.

Avery gazed at him, pleading for mercy. "Father... please..." she croaked, her voice brittle and weak. She desperately wanted to find any trace of compassion, anything to end this torture.

However, Lord Darmon's stony expression remained unchanged. "Progress requires sacrifice, daughter. You should feel honoured to further the Order's great work." His indifferent response extinguished Avery's last fluttering belief of awakening any humanity within him. Here, there was only ambition, devoid of mercy or love.

Drawing from the deepest well of her strength, Avery breathed out Lucien's name, each syllable a fervent, silent prayer. In the encroaching shadows nibbling at her vision's edge, she conjured the memory of his gentle smile, a solitary beacon in the engulfing darkness. As the tendrils of unconsciousness started to wrap around her, teetering on the verge of surrender, she could nearly make out the faint echo of Lucien's voice—a soothing whisper in the recesses of her dimming awareness.

Avery clung to that faint sound with all the fibres of her being. It was the escape connecting her to the world outside this nightmarish chamber, the only thread binding her to Lucien and the love they shared. Every whisper of his voice, even through the darkness, felt like an embrace, a promise that they would be together again.

With every infusion of demonic blood, Avery's animosity toward her father burned like a smouldering ember within her. The once-conflicted resentment of an abandoned daughter had transmuted into fiery contempt for the man who could mercilessly subject his own flesh and blood to such torment.

With sudden clarity, Avery realised Lucien was her genuine family now. For him, she would fight with every remaining ounce of her humanity. It was his love that anchored her, gave her strength to resist her father's wicked designs, and would guide her back to the light.

Despite the agonising injections, Avery's abhorrence for her father festered like an infected wound, poisoning her heart and spirit. She was aware of the destructive nature of harbouring hatred, knowing well its ability to corrode the soul. Yet, confronted with such torment, she found herself unable to suppress the surge of anger within her.

To her, there was no justification for the insatiable ambition that had utterly consumed her father. The man who had once been her parent now stood as a monstrous figure, lost in the darkness of his own desires.

There had been a time when she dared to dream that he might love her if only she proved herself worthy, achieving the impossible feat of making him proud. She had tried desperately to earn his affection. Through the trials she endured, Avery came to see the futility of her efforts. Her father was incapable of such emotion; incapable of love.

As the poison of demonic blood coursed through her veins, Avery's resolve solidified. She swore to herself that even if she emerged from this ordeal as a monster, she would never be her father's obedient puppet. She would sooner embrace death than kill for the Order and become a pawn in his malevolent games.

Avery clung to that defiant spark within her. She would show mercy where Darmon showed none. She would hold on to the memory of her humanity, refusing to let the darkness engulf her.

Gathering her determination amidst the relentless agony, Avery shifted her focus to meet the gaze of the man who had formerly held the role of her father, the figure standing above her. Her voice, barely more than a croak, betrayed her desperation. "Why?" she implored. "What has led you down this path?"

For a fleeting moment, something crossed Lord Darmon's face. Uncertainty, perhaps? Remorse? But it was quickly replaced by an impenetrable mask of indifference.

"You seek understanding where none exists," he replied coldly. "I act under reason. My duty is to further the Order's power and secure what is rightfully ours."

Avery shook her head bitterly. "No... there must have been a time when you were still human inside, before..." Her voice trailed off as she searched for any glimmer of humanity in him, a thread that could be tugged to bring her father back from the abyss.

However, Lord Darmon simply signalled to the demon, instructing it to continue the brutal infusions. As fresh waves of agony washed over her, Avery confronted a painful truth—whatever traces of humanity had once dwelled within him were long dead, devoured and decayed by the darkness that now shrouded him. He stood as the elder monster in the room, and that was something she couldn't alter.

Chapter 4

LUCIEN'S MIND TEEMED WITH DETERMINATION AS HE considered the forces they could rally for the impending battle. The urge to charge blindly for Avery's rescue warred with the need for a well-constructed strategy. He knew that a headlong rush into the Order's stronghold could spell doom for all of them.

Madame Leana's words brought him back to the present. Her gaze focused on some distant point as if foreseeing the events to come. "The witch Jade and the demon Ash will play pivotal roles. And, of course, your army of vampire knights, sired by both you and Vlad."

He felt a glimmer of hope. The knights, bound by loyalty to him and Vlad, were a formidable force. Their combined might could tip the scales in their favour.

With a determined nod, Lucien agreed. "I'll get them set for the attack as soon as it gets dark. With Jade, Ash, and your magic on our side, we can take down the Order's stronghold."

Madame Leana acknowledged him with a nod. "The pieces are aligning. Have faith."

Icy purpose surged through Lucien, quelling the turmoil of emotions that had roiled within him. He would leave no stone unturned, no plan unexecuted, to breach the stronghold, reunite with Avery, and vanquish the darkness that held her.

Departing from the ritual chamber, he wasted no time and made his way to the academy's training quarters. The atmosphere was charged with energy as his vampire knights diligently honed their weapons and clad themselves in armour etched with symbols of power. Every instance of metal scraping against metal, every glimpse of a blade meeting the whetstone, signified their commitment to the upcoming battle.

Lucien, embodying his commanding presence, scrutinised his army with a discerning eye. In the impending assault, every detail held significance. As he moved among them, he discerned unshakable obedience in their eyes and a fierce resolve to defeat the enemy. These vampires had been tempered in the crucible of loyalty, bound to their masters, and were prepared to instil fear in the hearts of those who dared to oppose them.

His knights responded with a collective thump of fists against their chests, a growl of acknowledgment reverberating through the training quarters.

Content with their preparations, Lucien left them to their tasks and entered the serene embrace of the Victorian garden nestled within the academy's grounds. Dappled sunshine filtered through the foliage. The melodic chirping of birds, and the overall tranquillity of the garden, sharply contrasted with the storm of turmoil awaiting him.

As he traversed the sunlit garden, Lucien sensed

the world holding its breath, bracing for the impending chaos and conflict. He endeavoured to reflect outward composure, though an inner tempest raged relentlessly.

Behind the veneer of measured calmness, fears clawed at him. What if their arrival proved too late? What if Avery's suffering had surpassed redemption? These dire concerns, too heavy to vocalise, lay buried beneath the weighty mantle of duty.

Kneeling amidst the blossoms, Lucien closed his eyes, conjuring an image of Avery's cherished countenance. His whispered prayer resonated with fervour, a silent plea to any deities that might be listening.

"Hold on, my love. When the sky turns crimson in the sunset, I shall come for you. I swear this, even if the forces of hell stand in my way."

Rising to his feet, he gazed upward, allowing the sun's warm rays to infuse him with steadfastness. The hour of destiny loomed, and faith and resolution became their celestial guides.

As he departed the tranquillity of the garden, Lucien sought Jade and Ash. In Jade's candlelit chambers, they awaited him with expectation, determination etched on their faces. Lucien approached them, speaking solemnly. "It's almost time. Are you ready?"

Jade met his gaze, her resolve unswerving. "We are prepared." Ash nodded.

Lucien retreated to his quarters, a sanctuary of solitude before the storm of battle. There, he dressed himself in his combat gear, each piece an indication of his readiness for the looming conflict. The black armour, adorned with intricate symbols of power and protection, embraced him familiarly, a reminder of the strength and resilience within. Each piece had been a gift from Vlad, bestowed with the promise of safeguarding the future.

In the quiet of his room, with the last rays of sunlight dancing through the windows, Lucien donned his helmet. His words, a soft but fervent prayer, filled the space. "Guide our forces swiftly, lend strength to my sword arm, and keep Avery from harm." His voice bore the burden of determination.

Emerging from his chambers, Lucien radiated an aura of hope and steadfast resistance. With every stride, his commitment to the mission solidified—the rescue of Avery from the shadowy depths that held her. It wasn't just a battle against foes; it was a quest to reclaim love and light from the jaws of darkness.

Chapter 5

AT DUSK, LUCIEN WAS MOUNTED ATOP HIS MAJESTIC white stallion, with Jade and Ash by his side. The gathered rescue forces stretched out before him, an army of vampire knights, armoured and vigilant.

Madame Leana, her presence imposing, sat on her own steed at the rear. As the sun dipped below the horizon, she began her incantations, tracing arcane symbols that shimmered with mystic power.

A portal to the forest outside Garmarth Castle tore open before them, reality itself bending to their will. Lucien raised his mithril sword, projecting his commanding voice to the waiting knights.

"This night we ride for justice! Onward!" With the forceful battle cries of his knights, they charged, crossing the supernatural threshold.

The quest to save Avery had begun. Failure was not an option. Lucien's focus was squarely on the path ahead and the reckoning that awaited those who had dared to take his love from him.

Lucien rode through the swirling portal, the vampire legion following him with resolute loyalty. Ash, Jade, and Madame Leana flanked him on their steeds, their presence lending an air of ominous power to the scene.

Upon passing through the gateway, they emerged into the serene surroundings of a forest bathed in moonlight. Ancient trees stood around them, their leaves rustling in the gentle night breeze, whispering stories of battles and legends long past.

The moon's glow filtered through the canopy, casting a serene, otherworldly light on their surroundings.

In the distance, Garmarth Castle towered imposingly. Its massive walls, built from colossal stones that bore the scars of weather and war, stood defiant against the night sky. Each stone was a witness to the castle's storied past, etched with the wear of time and the echoes of ancient conflicts. In the moonbeam, these rugged boulders took on a ghostly pallor, giving the fortress an awe-inspiring yet sombre character.

Before this grand, historical backdrop, Lucien, his figure cloaked in the silvery sheen, signalled a halt with a raised gauntleted hand. His commanding presence was as steadfast as the castle itself, as his forces gathered in the shadow of its timeless walls.

"Heads up. The fortress is right in front of us," he declared. "Stick to the plan. Take down any opposition, but keep in mind, Darmon is our main target. I'll deal with him myself."

The vampire knights disappeared into the woods like shadows, each group heading to their assigned positions. Lucien turned to Jade and Ash, his eyes alight with fierce tenacity. "We shall draw their attention to the castle's gate. Let the assault begin."

Their steeds thundered forward as they approached the citadel's entrance. The sounds of clashing steel and battle cries already filling the night air as the first wave of knights engaged the bewildered guards. Lucien's doggedness was unshakable. They had reached the culmination of their relentless pursuit.

But as they neared the entrance, an unsettling feeling crept over Lucien. The guards seemed too few, and the fortifications around the Order's head-quarters appeared strangely lax. An uneasy suspicion churned within him, like a shadow hinting at a hidden threat.

Before a warning could escape his lips, the massive gates of Garmarth Castle exploded open, and an army of undead warriors surged forth, their malevolent eyes gleaming with hate. In their shadow, a monstrous demon, unlike any Lucien had ever seen, emerged from the keep's depths.

"Ambush!" Lucien's voice thundered, his sword flashing into his grip as the undead horde swiftly encircled them. Faced with this sudden onslaught, Jade and Ash conjured blistering arcs of magic and hellfire, while Madame Leana countered with her own arcane incantations.

But the demonic general leading this unholy

army only laughed, its voice grating like iron. "Little fools, did you think we wouldn't be prepared for your intrusion?"

As Lucien battled, his heart pounded with an icy dread. The sight before him revealed a grave miscalculation; the Order's forces were far more formidable than anticipated. Yet, driven by the burning need to save Avery, he refused to let despair take hold. With his fangs bared in fierce determination, he plunged into the fray, charging at the demon general with a reckless courage that disregarded the lurking dangers.

In the thick of battle, Lucien's sword clashed against the demon's jagged blades, sparks flying with each bone-jarring impact. His movements were a blend of attack and defence, a dance of desperate survival against overwhelming odds. Surrounding him, the battleground was a whirlwind of disorder and sorcery.

Jade, wielding her white magic with precision and grace, became a beacon of hope. Her spells illuminated the battlefield, turning advancing undead soldiers into piles of ashes, each burst of her power a testament to her strength.

Meanwhile, Ash was an unstoppable force, his form blurring into a whirlwind of destruction. He moved with a fierce intensity, his actions a fiery tempest that left nothing but scorched earth in his wake. His relentless assault ensured that any enemy daring enough to come near was swiftly met with a fiery end.

Amidst this chaos, Lucien fought on, each swing of his sword fuelled by the singular goal of reaching Avery, refusing to let anything stand in his way.

As Lucien battled fiercely on the ground, his attention was intermittently drawn to the aerial spectacle above. Madame Leana, a master of her craft, was a whirlwind of concentration and power amidst the chaos. Her hands moved with deft precision, tracing intricate patterns in the air as she cast potent counter-spells. These shimmering barriers of magic rose like protective domes above them, repelling and dissipating the dark spells hurled by the Order's sorcerers. Energy crackled in the atmosphere as her counter-magic clashed with the enemy's curses, producing bursts of light that illuminated the battleground.

On the ground, Lucien was a force to be reckoned with, his sword cutting a relentless swath through the legion of undead. Each swing of his blade sent enemies stumbling backward, their numbers momentarily thinning before him. The undead, with their lifeless eyes and gnashing teeth, surged towards him like a relentless wave, but Lucien met them with an unyielding determination.

As he fought, he moved ever closer to where Madame Leana was concentrating her efforts. Her presence shone as a ray of hope, pivotal in shifting the momentum of the battle. With each step, Lucien pushed through the horde, his mind singularly focused on breaking through to join forces with her, knowing that together, their combined strength could shift the balance in this perilous fight.

With a fierce thrust, Lucien impaled his sword into the demon's chest, causing the monstrous creature to stagger back, howling in agony. But there was no time to savour this momentary victory—the ambush still raged around them.

"We keep fighting!" Lucien roared, his voice cutting through the clamour. "For Avery!" Renewed by desperation, he sliced through the demon's legs before twirling to decapitate more opponents, his sword arm unfaltering.

Jade sent a pack of undead foes into fiery oblivion. "We'll never back down!" she declared defiantly. Madame Leana nodded silently, her eyes blazing as she summoned radiant bolts of heavenly fire.

Lucien barked out commands to his allies, resolute in his judgement to press forward. Somewhere within the castle, Avery awaited rescue, and he would fight, no matter what obstacles or terrors lay ahead.

He carved a path through the relentless forces that sought to block their advance, his sword a gleaming blur of deadly purpose. Despite the crushing burden of fatigue and injury, he refused to stop.

Madame Leana, not far from Lucien, unleashed a cataclysmic shockwave. The air trembled as her power surged forth, obliterating an entire battalion of undead warriors in a blinding explosion of energy. Despite this display of might, Lucien couldn't help but notice the grim truth; the enemy seemed endless. As quickly as one foe fell, another took its place, an unceasing tide of darkness.

Nearby, Jade and Ash stood back-to-back, an island in the storm of chaos. Their voices intertwined in a symphony of incantations, weaving protective wards to fend off the ceaseless onslaught of dark magic. Each spell cast was a battle in itself, a struggle to maintain their ground under the relentless assault. Lucien could see the strain on their faces, and the sheer effort it took to hold the line.

Amidst the clashing and spell casting, a daring plan began to crystallise in Lucien's mind. The battle was hanging by a thread, and desperate times called for desperate measures. What if he pushed his stallion to its limits, leaping over the spiked gates to infiltrate the fortress alone? The idea was fraught with peril, yet it beckoned to him with the allure of turning the tide.

With this thought, Lucien urged his white stallion forward. The horse responded with fervent energy, its hooves thundering against the ground. His hands clenched the reins tightly, his entire being focused on the daunting gates that loomed ahead. In that moment, the chaos of battle seemed to blur into the background. His heart raced, fuelled not only by apprehension of the unknown ahead but also by a fervent desire to reach Avery. Every fibre of his being was aligned towards that singular goal, driving him towards what could be the most perilous, yet decisive action of the battle.

The spiked gates approached with dizzying speed. With reckless abandon, Lucien shouted for his noble steed to leap. For one suspended, heart-pounding moment, they soared through the air. Then, the world exploded in a deafening cacophony as horse and rider crashed through the reinforced wood gates, sending a shower of splinters and debris flying.

Lucien was dashed from the saddle as his mount collapsed lifelessly to the ground. Every inch of his body throbbed with pain; every bone screamed in protest. But it was nothing compared to his burning need to reach Avery. His mithril armour was battered and blood oozed from multiple wounds, but he clutched his sword steadfastly.

Lucien, dishevelled and slightly disoriented, paused to take in his new, eerily quiet surroundings. The once familiar clamour of battle was conspicuously absent, replaced by an ominous silence that blanketed the castle's empty courtyard. He found himself at the core of the enemy's domain, yet an uncanny stillness prevailed, like the deceptive lull before a tempest. His heart raced with the anticipation of hidden dangers, the certainty of a trap lurking in the shadows.

Turning cautiously, his heightened senses strained to detect the slightest hint of movement or threat. "Show yourselves!" he demanded, his voice echoing defiantly against the ancient walls. Blood seeped from a cut on his forehead, but it did little to dampen his spirit. He marched forward, each stride a fusion of courage and unease, guiding him closer to the imposing entrance of the stronghold.

When he reached the massive oak and iron doors, Lucien summoned his remaining strength and heaved them open. The tortured screech of metal grated on his ears. As he stepped into the cavernous hall beyond, torchlight flickered, revealing a labyrinth of vacant corridors branching off in all directions. Where were the keep's forces? The ominous stillness sent shivers down his spine.

Lucien inhaled deeply, recognising a faint yet unmistakable scent—the sweet fragrance of Avery's skin. His preternatural senses came alive, guiding him toward her elusive trail. Though he knew it was likely a trap, he had no choice but to follow it.

His grip on his sword tightened as he stalked through the stone passages, guided solely by Avery's lingering fragrance. With each step, torchlight gradually gave way to consuming shadow. Yet he pressed on, relentless in his pursuit.

Finally, he arrived before a nondescript wooden door. It was here that the scent was strongest. Without hesitation, Lucien knocked it open and charged into the impenetrable darkness beyond, prepared to face any obstacle, any adversary who dared stand between him and his love.

"Avery!" he shouted, his voice ringing through the oppressive darkness. He braced himself for a confrontation, ready to battle any enemy that lurked. But what he heard in response was not the clash of swords or the hiss of dark magic. Instead, a weak cry pierced the shadows—Avery's voice, calling out from below.

Lucien froze, torn between relief and a mounting sense of dread as Avery's weak cry echoed. He spotted a cramped, spiral staircase that led downward, presumably into the foreboding castle dungeons. Without a second thought, he took the slippery steps two at a time, his heart pounding with urgency.

"Avery! Hold on!" Lucien called out as he descended into the clammy, oppressive darkness of the dungeon. Her voice led him through the serpentine passages, the rusty iron bars lining the way only increasing his determination.

Lucien's heart pounded as he raced through the shadowed corridors, finally halting before a massive wooden door. It was old and imposing, its surface etched with arcane symbols that seemed to pulse ominously in the dim light. Faint, muffled sobs seeped through the cracks, igniting a fierce determination in his chest. With a roar that echoed his inner turmoil, he channelled his dwindling strength and rammed the door off its hinges.

The room beyond was a dim cell, its air heavy with despair. In the gloom, Avery was a broken figure against the filthy wall, her wrists cruelly chained. Her face, once vibrant, was now drawn and pale, a stark testament to her suffering. But at the sight of Lucien, a flicker of life reignited in her eyes, a fragile flame of hope amidst her anguish. She attempted to stand, her words a hoarse murmur, "You came..."

Lucien's heart ached as he rushed to her, his arms enveloping her trembling form. His sword, an extension of his resolve, swiftly broke the chains that imprisoned her. "I swore I would find you," he whispered back, his voice a tender caress as he gently brushed her matted hair away from her face. Despite her frailty, Avery managed a weak smile, her spirit unbroken. "I never gave up hope."

Lifting her with utmost care, Lucien's emotions swirled with relief and joy. They moved through the castle, a labyrinth of shadows and silence, remarkably unimpeded. Holding Avery close, he navigated the deserted halls, her safety his only focus. Yet, the lack of resistance was unsettling, casting a pall of suspicion over their escape. The eerie absence of foes, the quiet ease of their departure, seemed too simple, too unchallenged. Lucien's senses remained on high alert, his mind racing with the possibility of unseen dangers lurking in the quietude of their escape.

Chapter 6

AS THEY EMERGED INTO THE IMPOSING HALL, A VAST expanse illuminated by flickering torches, an unsettling sound shattered the silence. A slow, deliberate clapping resonated, each echo weaving a haunting melody through the air. The hall, with its high ceilings and grandeur, suddenly felt oppressive, the shadows cast by the torches seeming to dance menacingly around them.

Lucien's heart sank as he scanned the room, his grip on Avery tightening protectively. Then, materialising atop the majestic staircase like a phantom from the darkest of nightmares, stood Lord Darmon. His aura was icy and foreboding, standing in sharp relief against the comforting warmth of the torchlight. His smile, wide and contemptuous, was a mocking sneer that sent a shiver down Lucien's spine.

Lucien's mind raced, his thoughts a tumult of anger, fear, and determination. Darmon's appearance was not just a physical threat but a psychological one, his clapping a sinister symphony that seemed to mock their efforts and undermine their hope. His towering presence in the grand hall heightened the seriousness of the moment, casting an ominous aura over them. Lucien felt a surge of protective instinct, his resolve hardening against the looming confrontation, even as his heart pounded with the uncertainty of what was to come.

"Well done," he sneered, his voice dripping with malevolence. "You've found my precious daughter.

But did you honestly believe I'd allow you to take her so easily?"

Lucien clutched Avery tighter and raised his sword, determination etched across his face. "Your hold on her is broken, Darmon. You've lost."

Darmon's smile grew wider, like a grotesque parody of glee. "Lost? My dear Lucien, the game has only just begun..." With a sinister gesture, he twisted his hand through the air and started chanting, his intentions chillingly clear.

Avery let out a piercing cry of anguish as her body transformed. Her once-pale skin turned a sickly shade of red. Grotesque horns erupted from her head, and demonic wings tore through her back. The insidious twist of Darmon's magic had turned her from a vampire into a fully manifested demon.

Her voice, now guttural and inhuman, hissed menacingly, "You will not have me..."

Lucien staggered back, horror etched across his face as Avery completed her transformation. The familiar contours of her once-beloved form were now twisted by demonic fury. She hovered in the air on ominous crimson wings, hissing with a frightening and otherworldly cadence.

Darmon's malevolent laughter echoed through the hall as he addressed the demonic incarnation of

Lucien's love. "Come, fulfil your purpose! Kill the fool who dared to steal you away!"

Lucien felt tension building inside him as he prepared to confront the sinister power that had taken hold of Avery. However, as she dived towards him, there was no glimmer of recognition in her obsidian eyes. The woman he had loved so dearly was no more.

With savage speed, Avery seized Lucien by the throat, effortlessly lifting him off the ground. He gasped for breath, his sword tumbling from his grasp. This abomination wore Avery's face, but it was devoid of her essence.

"Finish him!" Darmon's command rang out from atop the stairs. Lucien did not struggle or plead.

Lucien was gasping, the demonic claws around his throat squeezing tighter, each breath a battle against the encroaching darkness. Darmon's eyes gleamed with malicious satisfaction from afar, savouring the imminent defeat of the once indomitable vampire. Lucien's heart pounded with despair, his mind a whirlwind of regret and unfulfilled promises.

In this dire moment, the castle's doors burst inward, shattering the tense air with their explosive entry. Ash, a figure of wrathful vengeance, stood framed in the doorway, his body wreathed in dancing flames, his eyes burning with an intensity that matched the inferno surrounding him.

The hall reverberated with Ash's thunderous shout. "Avery, no!" His arm swept forward, unleashing a fearsome wave of hellfire magic. Avery, caught in its path, was flung across the room, away from Lucien. The sea of flames that followed appeared to engulf everything in its wake.

Lucien crumpled to the ground, air finally rushing back into his lungs. Ash was at his side in an instant, lifting him up. "Come on. We must fall back. The battle is slipping from our grasp!" he shouted, his words almost drowned by the deafening roar of the flames consuming the hall.

Lucien's gaze was fixed on Avery, his heart wrenching in his chest. "I won't. I have to get her back." His voice was a desperate whisper, a plea to a fate that seemed already sealed. But the relentless fire, a barrier as solid as any wall, had already ensnared them in its deadly embrace, separating him from Avery.

Ash's words were a harsh dose of reality amidst the chaos. "There's nothing to be done right now. Last time I checked, fire kills vampires, and I don't have enough power left to hold him off, protect you from the flames, and keep Avery from killing you while you try to rescue her."

Lucien's heart sank, torn between the instinct to save Avery and the need to survive. The realisation that he was powerless to change the course of events was a bitter pill to swallow. As he allowed Ash to lead him away, his last glance back was filled with a tumult of emotions—despair, love, and an unwavering vow to return.

Leaning heavily on Ash, Lucien staggered toward the exit, each step an effort against his crushing despair. The echoes of Darmon's enraged roars behind them served as a haunting echo of the turmoil they were escaping. The roar of the inferno and the demonic Avery, now just echoes as the doors swung shut, sealing the fiery turmoil inside.

They had made it out alive, but the victory was hollow, the cost immeasurable in Lucien's heart. The haunting vision of Avery, consumed by darkness and engulfed in flames, replayed relentlessly in his mind, feeding a profound sense of despair. He was tormented by the thought of her succumbing to that malevolent transformation, her fate now an agonising mystery.

Yet, in this bleak moment, Lucien couldn't ignore the fact that Ash's intervention had been their salvation. It had given them a fleeting opportunity to escape, to regroup and perhaps to continue their struggle against the Order's relentless evil. The battle, indeed, was far from finished, but the uncertainty of Avery's fate cast a long, dark shadow over any sense of purpose.

Once at a safe distance from the now-blazing castle, Ash allowed them a moment to pause. Lucien rested against a tree, its cool bark sharply contrasting with the intense heat and chaos they had just fled. His thoughts were a tempest of feelings— sorrow, remorse, and a resolute feeling of inadequacy. The burden of the night's occurrences weighed heavily on him, each breath feeling like a battle against the overwhelming tide of despair that threatened to consume him. The distant, dancing flames of the burning castle served as a sombre reminder of the fierce battle they had recently faced and the unclear journey that still awaited them.

The uncertain path ahead seemed to stretch endlessly into darkness as Ash broke the heavy silence. "What happened at the gates?" His voice was urgent, laced with concern. "One minute we were fighting, then you just disappeared!"

Lucien's response was a shake of the head, his eyes mirroring the depth of his despair. "It was a trap," he murmured, defeated. "Darmon... he turned Avery into something she's not. She didn't even recognise me." His words trailed off, lost in the haunting image of Avery, now a stranger under Darmon's dark influence.

Ash's hand tightened on Lucien's shoulder, a gesture of solidarity in their shared anguish. "We'll get her back, don't worry. I can open a portal back to the academy. We'll regroup with the others, then..."

His words were abruptly cut off by a thunderous explosion that shook the very ground beneath them. The night sky was illuminated as the entire fortress succumbed to the flames, sending a rain of debris cascading around them. Yet, amidst this chaos, Lucien's gaze was resolute, fixed on the hellish scene where the castle once stood. His thoughts were entirely fixated on Avery, ensnared within the raging inferno. A profound sense of failure engulfed him, more suffocating than the smoke that rose in billowing clouds.

At that moment, Lucien's entire world seemed to contract to the blazing inferno before him, where every flicker and flame symbolised his inability to save the one he held dear. The realisation that Avery, the person he had braved so much to rescue, was still in the clutches of darkness, was a torment that no physical wound could match. The path ahead was not just uncertain; it was a labyrinth of guilt, fear, and unresolved desperation.

BACK WITHIN THE SOMBRE WALLS OF THE ACADEMY, Lucien found himself in the imposing presence of the council. The room, usually a place of wisdom and strategy, felt oppressively heavy, its air thick with anticipation and unspoken questions. He stood there, a solitary figure at the centre, his posture reflecting the immense burden he carried.

As he recounted the events of the disastrous assault, his voice was steady, but the underlying tremor of emotion was unmistakable. Every word he uttered reverberated throughout the chamber, underscoring the significance of their unsuccessful mission. The council members, their brows furrowed and expressions sombre, paid rapt attention, their silence casting a weighty pall over the room.

The suffocating cloak of failure bore down on Lucien, its weight constricting his chest with each breath. Every council member's gaze seemed to pierce through him, searching for answers or perhaps laying blame. The air was thick with disappointment and the bitter tang of defeat.

Lucien's recounting was more than just a report; it was an admission of his deepest fears and regrets. He spoke of the fierce battle, the unexpected strength of the enemy, and the heart-wrenching moment of Avery's transformation—a moment that replayed in his mind with painful clarity. As he spoke, his hands clenched and unclenched at his sides, a physical manifestation of his inner turmoil.

In that room, under the inquisitive eyes of the council, Lucien felt the full magnitude of what they had lost. It wasn't just a battle; it was a blow to their cause, to their hope, and to his heart. With each uttered word, the atmosphere chilled, and it felt as though the walls were tightening, echoing the squeeze within his soul.

"You never should've charged in alone," Ash said, his anger cutting through the air like a blade.

Lucien bristled, a defensive fire igniting within him as Jade chimed in. "Ash is right; that was too reckless."

Clenching his fists, Lucien retorted, "I did what I had to! I won't abandon Avery."

Vlad raised his hands diplomatically, but Lucien saw the clear divide among them. They thought he had jeopardised everything. They couldn't comprehend his need to reach Avery, no matter the peril.

Madame Leana watched pensively, her eyes reflecting the deep contemplation of a strategist. Lucien hoped desperately that she understood his motivations when no one else seemed to.

Alessandra's voice, sharp and decisive, cut through the tension. "Enough arguing! It wastes time and focus. We reformulate the strategy and strike back."

Ash and Jade had the grace to look ashamed, acknowledging the wisdom in Alessandra's words. Lucien knew she was right—unity was crucial, regardless of their internal disagreements. Yet doubt gnawed at him relentlessly. Had he doomed their mission?

Self-doubt twisted in Lucien's gut. Ash and Jade's accusations were a constant echo. If only he had adhered to the plan, Avery might be safe now. Instead, his impulsiveness could have condemned her. Lucien silently begged Avery's forgiveness, desperately praying it was not too late to reclaim her. But doubt tore at his confidence like a wolf toying with wounded prey.

The council room buzzed with uncertainty. Alessandra, though still recovering, suggested, "What if we hit them from multiple sides? It might overwhelm them."

Vlad gently intervened. "My love, let us handle the planning for now. You need more time to heal."

Alessandra objected, but Lucien observed the subtle trembling of her hands, a stark reminder of the recent pain. The ordeal was still too fresh.

Reluctantly, Alessandra eased back into her chair, acquiescing to Vlad's wisdom. Lucien's admiration for her willpower to contribute despite recent trials deepened.

Shaking off his doubts and getting his head back in the game, Lucien was determined. "We've got to save Avery. I'm not giving up on her—it's not too late to change things. No way I'm letting the shadows take her without one heck of a battle."

Amidst the ongoing discussions, Lucien couldn't shake a despairing thought. *Can any of us fully recover from the scars this evil left? Even if we defeat the dark minions ruling the Order, these haunting memories and trauma seem destined to linger, casting shadows over our lives forever.*

As Lucien tried to focus on strategizing their next steps, his thoughts kept returning obsessively to the unsettling image of Avery's transformation into a demon. The grotesque details were etched into his memory—the guttural voice, the obsidian eyes, and the leathery wings emerging from her back.

A wave of nausea swept over Lucien as he recalled the moment she had seized him by the throat with supernatural strength, poised to end his life at her father's command. His fingers instinctively went to his neck, vividly remembering her crushing grip.

Was the woman he loved truly lost to him now? Was there a sliver of hope that the real Avery remained buried deep within the hellish shell Darmon had forced upon her?

These lingering uncertainties threatened to shatter Lucien's determination. Yet, he desperately clung to one fragile lifeline—the memory of Avery briefly emerging from the castle flames returned to her vampire form. In that fleeting moment, he had glimpsed recognition in her eyes once more.

That fragment of belief was all Lucien needed—the faintest glimmer that he could reach the real Avery again. He vowed to traverse the fires of hell a thousand times if it meant saving her.

Chapter 7

IN THE OPPRESSIVE GLOOM OF HER CELL, AVERY existed in a limbo of nightmares and fractured memories. The concept of time had dissolved into a meaningless haze, her only anchor the flickering recollections of Lucien's love. It seemed like countless lifetimes had passed since the day she was cruelly torn away under Darmon's dark command.

The cell, with its chilling, solid stone walls, had become a world of endless night. Her spirit, though battered, clung to the faintest glimmers of hope, like a drowning person clinging to a life raft in a stormy sea. Every moment was a struggle against the encroaching despair, against the shadows that sought to erase the warmth of her past.

Suddenly, the distant, muffled sounds of combat pierced her numb consciousness. The clangs and cries, the symphony of a battle raging beyond her prison, sparked a dim, flickering curiosity. But then, cutting through the cacophony like a ray of light through darkness, came Lucien's voice. It was a sound she feared she'd never hear again, a powerful, familiar call that resonated with all the love and desperation of their bond. His voice acted as a soothing salve for her wounded soul, assuring her that she remained in his thoughts, never abandoned or isolated.

Disoriented, Avery struggled to lift her head, the effort monumental after endless hours of desolation. Her eyes, heavy with despair and weakness, slowly focused on the doorway. And there he was—Lucien, his presence a beacon in the endless night of her captivity. His features, etched with concern, love, and pure determination, were the most beautiful sight she could have ever imagined.

Witnessing him and catching her name on his lips ignited a spark of hope that ran deep within her. It was a fragile, trembling flame in the over-whelming darkness, yet it was enough to stir a reminder of life beyond these stone walls, of love waiting to be reclaimed.

"You came..." Avery's voice barely reached a whisper, a fragile utterance that appeared to bear the burden of all her suffering. As Lucien moved swiftly to her side, his every action spoke of urgency and care. With deft movements, he shattered the chains that had bound her, the sound of breaking metal ringing like a clarion call of freedom in the dismal cell.

As soon as the shackles released her, a wave of relief swept through Avery. It was a mild, calming wave that appeared to infuse vitality into her weary body. The cold, hard reality of her imprisonment seemed to momentarily fade as the warmth of hope and deliverance enveloped her.

In Lucien's presence, Avery felt a flicker of strength returning to her. His familiar face, etched with worry and fierce determination, was a sight that she had replayed in her mind countless times during her darkest moments. Just as he had vowed, he had located her, standing as a symbol of love and resilience amidst the depths of despair.

Lucien's eyes, filled with an emotion that spoke volumes, locked with hers. In that gaze, Avery saw not just the man she loved, but her saviour, her anchor in a storm that had threatened to swallow her whole. The awareness that he had braved uncharted perils to find her stirred appreciation and wonder in her heart.

In the safety of his presence, the horrors of her captivity seemed to recede, if only for a moment. Avery, though weak and worn, felt a resurgence of hope and an indomitable will to survive, to return to the world she knew, the world where Lucien's love was her guiding star.

Their reunion, a fleeting sanctuary in the abyss, was abruptly shattered. Avery's blood turned to ice when she beheld Darmon's sinister emergence, grinning malevolently like a puppet master revelling in his twisted play. She tried to warn Lucien, her voice a desperate plea, but then agony, an inferno of torment, seized her.

It was as if molten lava, searing and relentless, was coursing through her veins, reshaping her from the inside out. The last thing she saw through eyes blurred with tears was Lucien's distraught face etched with helplessness at witnessing her transformation.

Then, as though dragged into a tempest of anguish, Avery's consciousness seemed to retreat behind a wall of fire and rage. A demonic force, an insidious puppeteer, took control. The comforting embrace of nightmares replaced the fleeting solace of Lucien's presence, and she tumbled back into the abyss of her tortured dreams.

Trapped in the demonic form her father had cruelly forced her into, Avery experienced the overwhelming sensation of her consciousness being suppressed. It was like sinking helplessly in deep water, painfully aware of her surroundings yet completely powerless, as some dark force manipulated her body against her will.

Lucien's anguished countenance emerged like a spectre through the haze of rage clouding her mind. His silent plea seemed to reach out to her, a desperate call for the Avery he once knew. Instead of responding, alien words spilled from her lips, forming threats in a guttural distortion of her own voice.

Horror seized Avery as she sensed her monstrous

new form, a vile extension of her own being, lifting Lucien into the air by his throat. Her talons dug into his vulnerable flesh, and though she screamed internally for the malevolent force controlling her to cease, it only tightened its grip.

Mercy arrived as a sudden blast of flames knocked her away from Lucien. She collided with the unforgiving stone, momentarily stunned. The iron grip on her mind and body relinquished its hold, but only slightly.

In that fleeting moment of respite, Avery clung desperately to the sliver of free will that remained. She struggled to wrest back dominance, determined to show Lucien that the true essence of her being still lived under this hellish exterior.

Unable to articulate externally, she concentrated all her energy on their psychic bond, mentally projecting her desperate cry: *Lucien! I'm still here, trapped inside this thing! Please, don't leave me...*

The hope that he somehow heard her agonised internal plea was the sole lifeline preventing Avery from succumbing entirely. She knew that if she allowed this malevolent force to seize complete control, the last flicker of her true self would be extinguished.

Avery persisted in her futile struggle, attempting

to push back against the encroaching darkness that whispered insidious promises in her mind.

The tenuous connection with Lucien's mind snapped abruptly, leaving her in a disorienting whirl as she soared through the blazing corridors of the castle. When the demonic force that now controlled her body crashed into them outside, a sinking realisation accompanied the horror—Lucien was gone.

Deep within the murky confines of her besieged mind, Avery faintly perceived Ash hauling a bruised and weary Lucien to his feet. His urgent shouts were like distant echoes, struggling to penetrate the dense fog of her altered consciousness. A sense of desperation gripped her heart as she helplessly watched her potential saviours step through a glimmering portal, their figures dissolving into nothingness.

Inside, Avery's soul screamed, "Come back!" Her internal cries of anguish echoed through the desolation of her mind, but they were unheard, lost in the void that her existence had become. The portal sealed shut, trapping her in a distorted reality, a captive within her own twisted existence.

Around her, the remains of the battlefield lay in smouldering ruin, a haunting landscape that mirrored the chaos within her. The sensation of abandonment was overwhelming, a crushing blow to her already fragile state. Lucien, her beacon of hope, had disappeared, leaving her stranded in a monstrous existence, tormented by the remnants of her humanity.

In that desolate moment, Avery felt the true depth of her transformation—an existence trapped between two worlds, unable to reach out or be heard. The realisation that she was now alone, a lone figure amidst the ashes of destruction, was a haunting and inescapable truth. Engulfed in a tumult of confusion and despair, her mind desperately held onto the diminishing memories of Lucien and her past life, a vivid contrast to the grim and monstrous existence she was currently enduring.

IN THE AFTERMATH, DARMON APPROACHED HER corrupted figure, still kneeling in the dirt. Through the eyes of the monstrous creature she had become, Avery beheld his smug smile.

"It seems your dear hero has abandoned you," Darmon gloated, his icy voice dripping with satisfaction. "Now, let us leave this worthless place behind. I have grand plans for utilising your new talents..."

If Avery had control of her grotesque features, tears of abject misery would have streamed down her face. However, all she could do was watch helplessly as Darmon opened a portal, spiriting them away to some ominous, unknown destination.

Avery drifted into the depths of desperation as Darmon seized her mutated form, propelling them through the portal. They emerged in a crumbling, overgrown courtyard surrounded by broken walls adorned with dead vines.

Ominous clouds veiled any trace of sunlight, casting the ruined castle grounds in muted grey hues. Avery discerned a crooked, partially collapsed tower, its top rotunda conspicuously absent in the desolate landscape.

"Welcome to Château de Draven, my dear," Darmon declared, his voice oozing with sinister delight. "A jewel of French nobility, now a forsaken relic. Quite fitting, don't you think?"

Avery shivered inwardly at his words. The desolate ruin mirrored her own inner emptiness. Imprisoned in her demonic form, she was helpless as Darmon led her towards the castle's main structure.

The remnants of the once-grand chateau loomed

around them, its silence haunting. The damp, musty air clung to them, heavy with the ghosts of its splendid past. Despite her monstrous shell, Avery recoiled from the eerie aura of decay.

"A bit of training before we begin," he mused, leading them into a spacious overgrown courtyard. Nature, relentless in its reclamation, had woven a tapestry of moss and ivy over the once-proud stones, a sharp difference from the demonic presence that now defiled the historic grounds.

Therein waited a dozen hulking, red-skinned demons armed with jagged spears—a personal guard summoned from some hellish domain. At Darmon's approach, they eagerly stomped hoofed feet, awaiting his command. The courtyard, once a backdrop for refined gatherings, now played host to a sinister spectacle.

Darmon smiled coldly. "Now, let us see a demonstration of what my creation can do."

At those chilling words, Avery felt the demonic persona controlling her raise up to its full, imposing height. Massive wings unfurled, and vicious talons were bared, a murderous look crossing its stolen features. The grotesque transformation sent shivers down Avery's spine, her own consciousness trapped within the monstrous shell.

The enthralled demons surrounding them brandished their weapons with brutal delight at the sight of their target. Avery could only scream soundlessly, her silent cries echoing her despair at the horrors about to be unleashed.

Unable to control the mutated flesh forced under Darmon's sway, Avery watched her demonic shell tear through the guards with feral bloodlust. Every pleading thought for restraint went unanswered, and the courtyard became a gruesome theatre of violence. The stench of blood and the grotesque tableau of ragged corpses lingered in the air.

Darmon watched from the sidelines, a fascinated spectator as the last demon fell. His smile, a twisted enjoyment of the violence he orchestrated, sent chills down Avery's spine.

Clutching the amulet that commanded her, Darmon's actions filled her with terror, knowing the monstrous power she possessed was only the beginning of a greater wave of suffering to come.

In the slaughter's aftermath, Avery numbly watched Darmon seize control of her once more. As he pulled them deeper into the shadowy ruins of Château de Draven, her thoughts turned anxiously towards Lucien.

She knew he would try to find and somehow

save her, driven by love and guilt to redeem his failure. Part of her desperately hoped for that miraculous rescue, yet the practical part of her mind feared what wrath her warped body might unleash if he confronted her again.

She existed now as neither vampire nor demon, but an abominable hybrid, a monstrous convergence of both species. Within her, the apex abilities of vampires and demons intertwined creating a volatile mix. Her blood pulsed not only with vampiric impulses but also with deeper, primal, demonic desires for violence and devastation.

The thought of Lucien facing her under Darmon's influence haunted her. The insatiable lust for brutality within her would overwhelm the remaining traces of mercy. In this new shell, restraint was non-existent, replaced only by a feral hunger to destroy everything in its path. Dread consumed her as she contemplated the possibility of Lucien becoming another casualty in the wake of her horrific rampage.

Avery blinked back helpless tears, the physical manifestation denied by her transformed state. She wished desperately that Lucien would let her go, to forget the grisly entity his love had become. Death, she believed, would surely be kinder than the twisted ruin Darmon had made of her.

Avery sensed the monstrous strength granted by her warped hybrid bloodline, far exceeding the capabilities of either parent race alone. The vulgar display against Darmon's demon guards had only scratched the surface of the savagery these newfound talents could unleash.

Avery was deeply terrified by this realisation—the knowledge that beneath her usurped flesh lay a destructive force, dormant yet ready to be unleashed for whatever wicked intentions Darmon had planned.

When Darmon deemed her 'training complete,' Avery feared for wherever he might unleash her as his weapon. She knew no defences would hold against the embodiment of terror he envisioned–an unchained beast of hellfire, chaos, and retribution incarnate.

Avery desperately hoped that Lucien would not attempt to face that nightmare creature, despite his yearning to reclaim the lover cruelly taken from him. The thought of her mutated hands rending his heart from his noble chest, her demonic blood revelling in his grisly end, was a vision too agonising for her to bear.

Chapter 8

AVERY'S STEPS WERE HEAVY WITH DESPONDENCE AS Darmon guided her through the dilapidated corridors of the castle. Her eyes, once vibrant, now reflected a deep, unspoken sorrow. Each command from Darmon was like a physical burden, pressing down on her with the grim awareness of her own helplessness. Stepping into an empty, unsettling chamber, the weight of his ambitious schemes appeared to grow, enveloping her in a tangible cloak of desolation.

In the midst of this bleak march, something unexpected stirred within Avery. A subtle shift, a momentary loosening of the invisible shackles that bound her will to Darmon's. Her eyes widened slightly, a spark of hope igniting in their depths. Tentatively, she tested this newfound slack in her mental bonds, pushing against the limits of Darmon's faltering control.

Darmon, absorbed in his own thoughts, was caught off guard as Avery's monstrous form jerked violently, her talons scraping against the ancient wall, leaving deep scars in the stone. His eyes widened in shock and anger. "You dare resist?" he spat out, his hand scrambling for the amulet, seeking to tighten his grip on her once more.

The moment was brief, but it was a crack in the fortress of Darmon's control, a glimmer of rebellion that shone through the darkness of Avery's captivity. It was a silent battle of wills, her newfound resistance clashing against his hurried attempts to reassert dominance.

Avery's movements towards the door were frantic and uncoordinated, her wings flailing wildly, knocking over fixtures in her path. There was no plan in her mind, no strategy—only the primal urge to escape, to seize this fleeting opportunity for freedom.

But as she lurched desperately across the chamber, a sudden, excruciating pain shot through her. Darmon's magic, like invisible chains, snapped back with a vengeance, snatching away her brief glimpse of liberty. Her body froze mid-step, the freedom she had just begun to taste cruelly snatched away.

She crumpled to her knees, the agony rendering her helpless. The brief illusion of escape shattered, leaving her once again ensnared in her monstrous form, a puppet to Darmon's whims.

Darmon approached, his voice dripping with scorn. "Did you truly think you could escape me?" He stood above her, his gaze cold and contemptuous as Avery trembled under his stare, a victim of his unrelenting dominance.

"Perhaps I have been too lenient," he mused, his eyes flashing dangerously. "Allowed you to cling to some futile hope of defiance." He leaned closer, his presence menacing. "But no more. Now, you will learn what it means to be truly obedient." His words were a chilling promise of the tighter grip and harsher dominion that awaited her.

Darmon reached into the depths of his robes, his fingers wrapping around the handle of a ceremonial dagger. As he pulled it out, the strange glyphs etched into the blade seemed to come alive, twisting and turning in a sinister dance. "Pain has been a useful teacher," he said, his voice cold and calculated. "Let's resume our lessons."

With a wave of his hand, Darmon's magic forced Avery's monstrous arm to extend, bending her will with ruthless efficiency. Avery watched in horror as he positioned the dagger above her outstretched hand. Then, with deliberate slowness, he pressed the blade into her flesh, carving through skin and sinew. The precision of the cut was terrifying, the pain indescribable.

A silent scream tore through Avery as her body convulsed in agony. The torture she was enduring was unimaginable, beyond any physical pain she had previously known. Darmon loomed over her, his eyes gleaming with cruel satisfaction. The sight of her suffering seemed to bring him a perverse joy.

Avery shook uncontrollably, trapped in her monstrous form and at the mercy of her captor. She was powerless to stop him as he meticulously peeled back the skin of her palm, each movement calculated to inflict maximum pain. Mute and agonised, she could do nothing but endure the relentless cascade of injuries, each one a brutal lesson in 'obedience.'

Eventually tiring of focusing on just her warped hand, Darmon circled Avery's hunched demon form. "I think the wings could use some of our attention..." he purred, placing one hand almost gently between the leathery appendages extending from her spine.

Without warning, scorching pain shot through Avery's entire back. The razor-edged dagger carved mercilessly into the sensitive flesh and thin bones, flaying wings from the body in excruciating degrees.

She would have wailed to the heavens if her jaw were her own. But Avery could only suffer in silence as the torture seemed to last for eternity. Finally, she teetered at the edge of her endurance, ready to plunge into that black oblivion.

Relief, however, remained elusive. Darmon applied just enough healing to keep her conscious, only to continue inflicting atrocious new pains on her mutilated form. In those moments, Avery couldn't help but think that death would have been a far more merciful fate.

As Darmon's relentless torment continued, Avery

found herself paralyzed, unable to escape the physical agony he wrought upon her. In these unbearable moments, her only solace was to withdraw into the deepest recesses of her mind, seeking shelter in the sanctuary of her memories.

There, in the quietude of her psyche, she conjured images of Lucien, each memory a precious balm to her ravaged spirit. In her mind's eye, she pictured the strength and solace of his embrace, its warmth a vivid contrast to the harsh, cold reality she was currently enduring. Lucien's gentle touch soothed her pain, his whispered words of love and reassurance echoing like a sweet melody amidst the cacophony of her suffering.

This mental refuge, built from cherished moments and tender recollections, became Avery's fortress against the onslaught of Darmon's sadistic magic. Clinging to these fragments of happier times, she found the strength to endure, to resist being completely consumed by despair. Within this sanctuary of her mind, Lucien stood as a shining pillar of hope, symbolising a love that continued to glow vibrantly, undimmed even by the darkest moments.

As the torment stretched on endlessly, Avery's newfound resilience seemed to silently defy her captor. Darmon scowled, intensifying his attacks, but was met only with passive stoicism.

"What manner of sorcery is this?" he eventually snarled, confusion mixing with frustration as Avery endured silently. "You dare withstand me so insolently?"

Darmon, enraged by Avery's lack of response, raised his hand in a furious gesture, signalling an even harsher punishment. But fate intervened; his magic, unstable and erratic, suddenly recoiled. The walls trembled, and with a thunderous crash, debris rained down, trapping him beneath. Half-buried in rubble, his plan had dramatically backfired.

Pinned beneath the rubble, Darmon's initial fury quickly transformed into a barrage of threats and vulgar outbursts. Yet, as his predicament became more dire, his furious outbursts gradually turned into desperate bargaining and pleading, laying bare his true state of helplessness amidst this unforeseen turn of events.

Avery's eyes widened in disbelief, struggling to process this unexpected turn. Despite her scars and pain, felt a glimmer of hope flickering within her. Maybe, just maybe, the tide was turning.

"Come now, release me... we shall let bygones be bygones." He appealed to Avery's motionless form under his control. "Did I not gift you your magnificent power? Together, no one could oppose us!"

If she could have spat at his feet, Avery would have. But outwardly she could only observe his humiliation silently. Inside, her mind raced.¾ Was there a chance now for escape?

Avery gathered her willpower, concentrating on coaxing any movement from her transformed, unwilling body. Darmon's iron grip had weakened, a crack in his control now evident. This was her chance, and she knew she had to take it, no matter the cost.

Summoning all her strength, she managed to lift a heavy clawed limb. Each movement was an arduous battle, but inch by painstaking inch, she dragged herself towards the possibility of escape. Darmon's voice echoed behind her, a cacophony of threats that eventually faded into hoarse, desperate pleas.

Away from Darmon's gaze, Avery suffered intense pain with every motion. Her wings were tattered, her bones broken and twisted from relentless torture, yet she persisted. Her progress was slow, driven by a primal instinct for survival, like a wounded animal seeking the sun's comforting warmth.

At last, her bloodied palm felt the touch of grass, offering a striking contrast to the cold stone she had just left behind. Sunlight enveloped her battered form, a gentle caress against her wounds. In this moment of fragile peace, a flicker of hope ignited within her. Maybe, just maybe, she had reclaimed a part of her soul in this desperate flight for freedom.

But a chorus of guttural shouts shattered that dream. A pack of Darmon's demon sentries bounded over, roughly seizing Avery's prone form. Helpless once more, she retreated into her mind as they hauled her back down the stone steps into darkness.

Avery lay broken at the feet of her captor, his enraged voice filling the air. His fury was palpable, berating her for her daring but doomed attempt to escape his dominion. He mocked her hope, scoffing at the idea that light could ever penetrate the perpetual darkness of his reign.

The sound of chains rattled through the gloom as they were mercilessly tightened around her, forcing her battered body to stand upright against the cold, damp wall of the castle's depths. The room was a tomb-like void, save for the two of them—captor and captive, creator and unwilling creation.

In this desolate place, Avery's spirit remained her only unbroken attribute. Her body might have been chained, but her defiant gaze remained unbending, a silent testament to her indomitable will.

Darmon's smug laughter reverberated off the uncaring stone walls, pleased with his restoration of order from chaos. He turned to Avery, his voice dripping with venomous smoothness, a predator relishing his control over his trapped prey.

"Now then, my dear... where were we?" Darmon's talons traced a path down Avery's scarred cheeks, each touch sending a wave of revulsion through her. His gesture was a chilling reminder of the never-ending torment that awaited her.

"Did you really think a fleeting moment in the sun could save you?" he taunted. "There's no escape. You're mine, in life and death."

His words, dripping with malice, ignited a defiant flame within Avery. Though weak, she lifted her bloodshot eyes to meet his, her gaze attempting to convey the contempt she couldn't voice.

Darmon's grin only grew at her silent challenge. "Ah, there's still some fight in you. Good!" he said with perverse delight. "It will be all the more satisfying to extinguish." His hand moved lower, his touch igniting a fresh wave of revulsion in Avery, a stark reminder of her helplessness in his vile presence.

"My lord!" came a sudden shout as a demon underling burst into the dungeon chamber uninvited. Darmon's claws tightened angrily around Avery's throat.

"What is it, fool?" he snapped, impatience etched across his face at the interruption.

The lackey trembled slightly under Darmon's baleful glare. "Surface forces requesting reinforcements. We are under attack!"

Darmon hesitated, then smiled slowly with sinister delight. "Well, now... it seems we have guests."

Chapter 9

LUCIEN'S FOOTSTEPS ECHOED IN THE COUNCIL chamber, each step a measure of his growing desperation. His mind was a whirlpool, circling tirelessly around one goal. Rescuing Avery. Days had passed since their failed attempt, but the image of her twisted into some demonic puppet was seared into his memory, replaying over and over.

Vlad, standing with his arms firmly crossed, broke the tense silence. "We need to find out where Darmon has hidden her," he said firmly. "Only then can we plan a new attack."

Seated at the table, Madame Leana nodded, her expression pensive. "My visions are clouded... fragments of old castle ruins, deep in a vast forest," she murmured, her fingers massaging her temples as if trying to dispel the fog of her elusive foresight.

Lucien halted, his frustration boiling over. "We can't just sit around!" he exploded, his voice a sharp crack in the tense atmosphere. "Avery could be suffering unimaginable things right now. We have to go after Darmon immediately!" His shout reverberated off the walls, his eyes, fraught with anguish, beseeching them to feel the urgency that was eating him alive.

In the midst of this charged air, Ash chimed in, his tone curious yet uneasy. "But how did Darmon even turn Avery into a demon? Is that something his magic can do?"

Vlad, pondering, stroked his chin thoughtfully. "To transmute someone so profoundly... it would require tremendous power and is likely irreversible."

His words, which carried subtle implications, hung in the air, adding to the weight of the challenging mission ahead.

"That kind of magic can scramble things, right? Make creatures violent, mindless," Ash pressed.

Lucien's body went rigid, a sharp pain clenching his chest as the stark reality of Avery's condition, so long pushed to the back of his mind, was laid bare in Vlad's words.

"Is there a way to control the demon Avery has become?" Vlad's voice was hesitant as he turned to Madame Leana.

The witch, her face etched with grave concern, slowly shook her head. "Tampering with such magic risks shattering her mind completely. We must focus on restoring Avery's soul, not further binding her to this cursed form."

Lucien's nod was bitter, his resolve tinged with pain. No matter how Avery had been transformed, he knew he owed it to her to fight for her freedom, for the return of her will.

As plans began to take shape around the table, a sudden spark of inspiration hit Lucien. "The manuscript!" he exclaimed, striding swiftly to a locked cabinet. With a sense of urgency, he retrieved an ancient text on demonology, its pages worn and tattered, a relic from the Old Church he had brought to the academy.

"This book," he said, holding it out, "is full of ancient spells for bending dark forces." The possibility hung in the air, a thread of hope. "Maybe it holds the key to undoing Darmon's work on Avery."

Ash leaned closer, his eyes gleaming with enthusiasm. "Holy hell! If I can ambush Darmon with some of these spells," he said, almost breathless with the prospect, "we might be able to free Avery from whatever he's using to control her."

Madame Leana traced a weathered demon sigil on the manuscript experimentally. "Unleashing such unstable magic will surely draw Darmon's full wrath. You must strike precisely while we occupy his attending forces."

Vlad crossed his arms. "Darmon has always coveted the power bound within these pages. By wielding it freely before him, we issue a brazen challenge none can ignore."

Lucien felt renewed conviction flow through the group, driving out despair. The manuscript imparted genuine hope. With it, Ash could be the wild card turning fortunes in their favour at long last.

As they studied their options, Jade spoke up

pensively. "What about the arcane map taken from Avery's cell? It could hold clues."

Lucien's expression grew intense, his brow creased with concentration. "I've had our top mystics go over it thoroughly," he said. "But Darmon's magic is elusive, leaving no discernible trail. We've already scoured the locations. They turned up nothing."

Jade leaned forward, her voice insistent. "But what about the physical contact Avery's demon form made? Couldn't there be some magical residue we can use for a location spell?"

Madame Leana, deep in thought, nodded slowly. "Possibly. Ash's connection to her might help us trace the faintest traces of her aura."

Ash flexed his hands, a determined glint in his eyes. "I'm ready to break through any magical shields that might be hiding her."

A flicker of hope ignited in Lucien's heart. With their combined strengths and the intricate web of magic they wielded, perhaps they could indeed penetrate the darkness shrouding Avery's whereabouts.

"Then we need to act fast," Lucien said decisively, a newfound determination in his voice. "The longer we wait, the deeper Darmon could bury her."

They gathered quickly in the ritual chamber,

driven by a palpable sense of urgency. The enigmatic map was spread out while Madame Leana began setting up the focal point of their spell, each movement precise and calculated. The air was thick with anticipation, the group united in their singular goal to unearth Avery from Darmon's clutches.

"Clouded forces obstruct my sight still around those castle ruins," she muttered.

Ash cracked his knuckles, unfazed. "We're getting Avery back."

Madame Leana passed him an engraved silver bowl. "Focus your power. Amplify Avery's essence to guide my vision."

Brow furrowing, Ash manifested swirling energy, the runic bowl glowing in his palms. Madame Leana worked swiftly, movements synchronising with the rising occult forces.

The very air thrummed with impending revelation. Lucien observed intently, hardly daring to breathe. Then Madame Leana gasped. The obscuring fog lifted at last.

"I see now! The western tower concealed below the broken ruins... shadowed dungeons where Avery lies captive."

Lucien gripped the table's edge at the news. "Can you open a gateway there directly?"

Madame Leana nodded, resolute. "The path is clear."

"Ready the knights. We embark at once!" Lucien added.

Madame Leana's divination triumph electrified the room with a new purpose. Finally, after tension-wracked days, they had pierced the veil to uncover Avery's location.

Lucien swiftly departed to rally the vampire knights for immediate mobilisation, his preternatural speed fuelled by single-minded urgency. Too much time had already been sacrificed while Avery endured torment and madness in the merciless dark.

Returning to the council chambers, Lucien found the rescue party gathered, faces set with solemn determination. Madame Leana stood ready beside a shimmering gateway and Jade gripped the Manual of Demonic Magic tightly with anticipatory focus.

Ash stepped forward, buckling on his engraved battle armour. "The legion is arrayed in full martial force, ready at your command." His steady voice left no doubt that failure could not be abided this time.

Lucien gave a sharp nod of acknowledgment. The hour for preparation had passed. Destiny called them to action. To cross the gateway into the belly of evil, retrieve their lost light, and salt the cursed earth that had defiled her.

Hand tightening on the pommel of his mythic blade, Lucien addressed them all. "We end this nightmare now!" Their answering cry shook the hall's rafters as, one by one, they stepped into the swirling portal that promised justice... or oblivion.

Chapter 10

As soon as they emerged from the portal, the rescuers found themselves in an eerie, overgrown courtyard surrounded by crumbly walls. Foreboding clouds obscured the sun, draping the castle grounds in subdued shades of grey. Broken walls covered in dead vines stood as silent witnesses to the citadel's former grandeur.

The air was heavy with the scent of decay, and the sounds of rustling leaves mixed with distant creaks and groans from the dilapidated structure. The courtyard, once a place of nobility and beauty, now lay in ruins, a forsaken remnant of a bygone era.

Lucien's heart tightened at the sight, the sombre atmosphere amplifying his sense of urgency. Guided by Madame Leana's divination, they had a purpose here—to rescue Avery from the depths of this run-down fortress.

Without exchanging words, the group moved forward with cautious steps. The uneven cobblestones beneath their feet echoed with the ghosts of a time long past. The castle seemed to come alive with whispers of the secrets it held, as if the stones themselves remembered the tales of joy and tragedy.

The grand entrance loomed ahead, a dark portal into the heart of their mission. Lucien inhaled deeply, sensing the heavy burden of responsibility resting on his shoulders. The time for deliberation had passed; now, they ventured forth into the haunted corridors, hoping to bring light to the shadows that clung to the castle.

As the group advanced through the dilapidated

corridors, eerie echoes accompanied their every step. The air grew thick with an otherworldly tension, signalling an imminent confrontation. Rounding a corner, they found themselves face to face with an ominous line of demonic guards, red-skinned and armed with jagged spears.

The demons stomped their hoofed feet in unison, their malevolent eyes fixed on the intruders. Lucien tightened his grip on his weapon, determination and apprehension etched on his face. Beside him, Ash stepped forward, his eyes aflame with magical energy.

With a swift motion, Ash raised his hands, and an intense burst of hellfire magic enveloped the demonic guards. The creatures writhed and roared as the flames consumed them, their forms disintegrating into smoke and ash. The corridor, once crowded with ominous figures, now stood empty, the echoes of the demons' demise lingering in the air.

Lucien spared a glance at Ash, who wore a steely expression. The infernal sentinels had been vanquished quickly, yet the aftermath of the confrontation hung heavily in the castle's shadowy corners.

As the group pressed on, the oppressive atmosphere of the fortification seemed to intensify.

The shadows clung to the ancient stones, whispering of forgotten secrets and malevolent deeds. Lucien led the way, his senses attuned to any sign of Avery's presence.

The corridor widened into a grand hall with a crumbling ceiling, revealing a night sky strewn with spectral constellations. Moonlight cast an ethereal glow on the worn tapestries that lined the walls. The group moved forward, guided by Madame Leana's divination.

Suddenly, they reached a set of ornate double doors adorned with symbols that seemed to writhe and pulse. Lucien exchanged a wary glance with Ash, who nodded, acknowledging the magical wards that protected whatever lay beyond.

Madame Leana's voice, soft yet resonant, filled the space, harmonising with the old magic around them. The symbols etched on the doors briefly shimmered with light, then faded away like vanishing fog. Accompanied by a creaking groan, the doors slowly opened, unveiling a vast chamber beyond.

As the group entered, the air thickened with a palpable malevolence. The chamber was dominated by a large, obsidian throne, upon which sat a figure shrouded in shadows. Darmon, the orchestrator of

Avery's torment, regarded them with cold amusement.

"You've come a long way to meet your demise," Darmon sneered, his voice echoing through the room. Lucien's jaw clenched, but he remained resolute. The time for confrontation had come.

Yet, as Darmon prepared to unleash his dark powers, Ash stepped forward once again. With a sweeping gesture, he conjured a vortex of hellish might, and the shadows recoiled. The sinister aura permeating the chamber appeared to tremble under the might of Ash's powerful magic.

The group prepared themselves for the looming clash between illumination and darkness, a pivotal struggle that would determine the destiny of Avery and the age-old fortress that had witnessed centuries of triumph and despair.

"Your dark games end here," Ash declared.

Ash's celestial vortex collided with the menacing forces that emanated from Darmon, creating a dazzling display of light and shadow. The clash echoed through the chamber, shaking the very foundations of the ancient fortress.

Lucien's gaze remained fixed on Darmon, his heart pounding with anxiety and anticipation. Avery's fate hung in the balance, and he could sense the ebb and flow of magical energies as the confrontation intensified.

The obsidian throne seemed to capture the swirling forces, magnifying Darmon's wickedness. Around him, shadows converged, morphing into tendrils that slithered out like ghostly serpents. The air hummed with a palpable charge of unfathomable power as the clash between Ash and Darmon reached its climactic point.

Amidst the whirling magical tempest, Darmon's voice cut through, dripping with arrogance. "Your feeble attempts to defy me are futile. Avery belongs to the darkness now, and you shall witness her transformation into a force beyond your comprehension."

Lucien gritted his teeth, determined not to be swayed by Darmon's taunts. The stakes were too high. He drew strength from the memory of Avery's true self, buried somewhere within the demonic shell.

Suddenly, the room trembled, and an otherworldly howl filled the air. The shadows recoiled as if repelled by an unseen force. Lucien squinted through the magical maelstrom, trying to discern the source of this disturbance.

Jade stood at the forefront, her eyes ablaze with a mystic light. She chanted incantations that seemed to resonate with the very essence of the stronghold. The ancient stones responded to her call, pulsating with a purifying energy.

As the dark tendrils entwining the throne began to unravel, a subtle shift occurred in Darmon's previously unshakable demeanour. His mask of confidence faltered, replaced by a fleeting glimpse of uncertainty. Sensing his moment, Ash intensified the power coursing through him, his hands swirling with an inferno of hellish energy. The vortex he conjured pushed against the looming shadows, lighting up the room with its fierce glow.

The moment Lucien stepped forward, the air in the chamber charged with anticipation. His sword, reflecting the chaotic light of the room, was more than just a weapon—it was an extension of his tenacity. He moved with fluid grace, each step measured and deliberate.

Darmon, recovering from his momentary lapse, responded with a sinister speed. He conjured a blade of pure shadow, its form flickering and unstable, yet deadly. The clash of their swords rang out, a discordant symphony of light and darkness.

Lucien's movements were a dance of precision and skill, honed from years of combat. He parried and thrust, his blade cutting through the air with a sharp hiss. Darmon countered with equal ferocity, his shadow blade a blur of motion, leaving trails of darkness in its wake.

Their swords met in a flurry of strikes and blocks, sparks flying with each contact. Lucien's arm muscles tensed with each swing, his focus absolute. Darmon, for his part, fought with wild, untamed energy, his attacks unpredictable and ruthless.

The sound of metal against shadow filled the chamber, echoing off the ancient walls. It was a battle not just of physical might, but of wills. The determined heart of a warrior against the corrupt power of a sorcerer. Each strike, each manoeuvre, was a testament to their opposing causes, a struggle that was as much about saving Avery as it was about defeating the darkness.

Chapter 11

THE CHAMBER BECAME AN ARENA WHERE LIGHT clashed against darkness, an explosive dance of opposing forces. Darmon, now visibly frustrated, watched his meticulously laid plans begin to crumble. The foundation of his control over Avery wavered under the assault.

"Bring her to me!" Darmon's voice echoed through the cavernous halls of the castle.

In response to his orders, a horde of demonic guards emerged from the shadows. Their grotesque forms, twisted by dark magic, moved with unnatural speed as they converged on Avery's location. The air crackled with malevolent force as the minions closed in.

Jade redoubled her efforts to dispel the lingering darkness. Her incantations echoed through the chamber, entwining with Ash's celestial magic. The very fabric of the castle seemed to resist the encroaching demonic forces. As the first of the guards lunged forward, Ash unleashed a surge of radiant energy. The hellfire struck the minions, causing them to writhe in agony. Some dissipated into shadowy remnants, while others recoiled from the sheer force of the onslaught.

Jade's magic intertwined with Ash's, forming a barrier that momentarily held the demonic minions at bay. Darmon's influence, however, was persistent, and the minions pressed on with unnatural tenacity.

"Lucien, be ready!" Ash called out over the tumult, his eyes blazing with celestial power.

With a swift and practised motion, Lucien swung his sword, fending off the advancing demons. He fought not only to protect himself and his allies but to create a barrier between Avery and the encroaching darkness.

Amidst the chaos, a haunting scream echoed through the chamber. It was Avery's voice, though distorted by the demonic influence. The minions, driven by Darmon's commands, were dragging her towards the throne where Darmon sat, still struggling against the combined forces of light arrayed against him.

Hearing the anguished scream, Lucien's determination deepened. He couldn't let Avery fall into Darmon's hands. Letting out a fierce battle cry, he launched himself into the fray, his sword slicing through the air, striking the demonic guards with lethal precision. Ash and the others were quick to follow, each tapping into their distinct powers to combat the advancing darkness.

The arcane energies clashed with the malicious forces, creating a chaotic spectacle of lights and shadows. Avery's struggles against the minions became more desperate as they tried to force her towards Darmon's throne. But Lucien fought with the strength of a man fuelled by love and desperation.

Madame Leana's eyes glowed with concentration and resolve. She chanted ancient incantations, seeking to sever the dark connection that bound Avery to Darmon's will. The very air seemed to ripple with the intensity of the magical battle.

As the minions closed in, Ash summoned a hell-fire barrier, creating a protective circle around Avery. The demonic entities recoiled, their twisted forms writhing in pain as they encountered the hellish might.

"Stay back!" Ash asserted, his voice resonating with a commanding presence.

But Darmon, sensing the turning tide, unleashed a surge of dark energy. The minions, empowered by their master's malevolence, redoubled their efforts. The battle reached a fever pitch, the crash of opposing forces echoing through the chamber.

Lucien fought his way through the demonic horde. His sword cleaved through the shadows, each strike aimed at protecting Avery. She continued to resist with every ounce of her being.

Madame Leana's incantations reached a crescendo, and a surge of mystical power enveloped Avery. As Darmon's hold faltered, Avery's resistance against the minions grew more forceful and noticeable.

With a final, resolute incantation, Madame Leana severed the dark link entirely. Avery, liberated from Darmon's control, collapsed to the ground, panting and disoriented. The demonic guards dissipated into shadows, leaving only echoes of their malevolence.

Silence descended upon the chamber, a stark contrast to the chaos that had just ensued. It was a haunting stillness, punctuated only by the laboured breathing of the weary rescuers and the faint hiss of dark magic fading into the ether. Lucien, his face a canvas of relief and worry, quickly moved to Avery's side. Gently, he gathered her into his arms, cradling her with a tenderness that belied the ferocity of the battle just fought.

As the oppressive shadows retreated, it became clear that this victory was more than a physical triumph. It was a fight for Avery's very soul, a fight against the consuming blackness that had threatened to claim her. In the wake of this hard-won battle, Darmon's presence loomed from his throne, his simmering rage palpable. His eyes, filled with malevolent fury, watched as his carefully laid plans came undone.

Blinded by a surge of protective fury, Lucien's gaze fixated on the cuts that marred Avery's delicate skin. The wounds inflicted during her struggles against Darmon's minions fuelled the fire of rage within him. With a speed that blurred the line between mortal and supernatural, Lucien darted toward Darmon.

In a single, fluid motion, Lucien closed the distance, his hand seizing Darmon's neck with an iron grip. The atmosphere crackled with tension as time seemed to freeze. Avery, still disoriented from the recent ordeal, looked on with a mix of surprise and concern.

With a swift and decisive movement, Lucien snapped Darmon's neck, the sickening sound echoing in the chamber. Darmon, once a puppet master revelling in cruelty, now slumped lifelessly, his malevolent gaze extinguished. The vampire's eyes glowed with a fierce, possessive protectiveness as he cast aside the vile orchestrator of Avery's torment.

In the aftermath of the battle, a profound silence enveloped the chamber. Lucien stood, his posture rigid, beside Darmon's still body. Each breath he took seemed to echo in the hushed air, a testament to the intense, vengeful struggle that had just concluded. The atmosphere hung heavy with the solemnity of their deeds, serving as a palpable reminder of the sacrifices undertaken for the sake of love and the quest for justice.

Avery, her own emotions a whirlwind, stepped toward Lucien with hesitant steps. The scars on her arms and back spoke volumes of her suffering, yet there was a subtle shift in her demeanour. As she looked at Darmon's fallen form, a faint sense of relief replaced the shadow of torment in her eyes.

The rest of the rescue team moved closer, their faces a complex tapestry of shock, relief, and quiet respect. Madame Leana observed them, her gaze mirroring a profound comprehension of the sacrifices and victories of their voyage.

Though the battle had left its scars, the chamber now thrummed with the undercurrent of a hard-fought victory. Lucien, a portrait of determination mixed with exhaustion, turned to face Avery. In his eyes, the fire of a man who had moved heaven and earth to save the one he loved still burned bright.

The journey was far from over, but in that suspended moment, the shadows seemed to retreat, granting respite to the weary souls who dared to defy the darkness.

As the adrenaline of the battle faded, Avery's

strength waned, and she collapsed into Lucien's waiting arms. He cradled her tenderly, love and concern evident in his touch, understanding the burden of her exhaustion and the haunting echoes of her suffering.

Lucien's gaze never left Avery's face, as if he could shield her from any lingering shadows with the sheer intensity of his protective stare. The others, their expressions weary, stood a respectful distance away, giving the reunited couple a moment of quiet connection.

Amid this poignant scene, Ash stepped forward. Understanding the need for a swift return to the academy, he wove the elaborate patterns of magic that opened the gateways between realms.

A soft, ethereal glow enveloped the group as the threshold manifested before them. Ash, his eyes focused and hands steady, maintained the spell. The portal became a doorway, a shimmering passage leading back to the familiar grounds of the academy where the war had initially begun.

With utmost care, Lucien lifted Avery into his arms, her head resting against his shoulder. Momentarily setting aside their fatigue, the rest of the group congregated around the couple, united by the triumph they had achieved.

Ash broke the silence. "Let's head back." His suggestion, simple yet comforting, pointed them towards the academy, a place now akin to a sanctuary in their minds compared to the sinister shadows they had just escaped.

As they crossed the threshold of the portal, the dilapidated castle and the echoes of their battle faded into nothingness. The journey between worlds was a mere instant, a swift blur of transition. Then, just as quickly, they were enveloped by the recognisable surroundings of the academy. Here, the air was different. It hummed with a sense of security and a soothing familiarity.

Avery, still cradled in Lucien's arms, smiled.

The portal closed behind them, leaving no trace of the harrowing journey they had undertaken. The school stood silent, but within its walls echoed the heartbeat of those who had faced the shadows and emerged, if not unscathed, then undeniably triumphant.

Chapter 12

WITH A SENSE OF URGENCY, LUCIEN CARRIED AVERY through the familiar halls of their sanctuary, his strides purposeful yet gentle. The heft of her body nestled in his embrace served as both a comforting presence and a stark testament to the trials she had faced. As they reached his chamber, he gently laid her down on the bed, a haven far removed from the malevolence they had left behind.

Alessandra, ever practical and composed, entered the room after them. Her keen eyes assessed Avery's condition, registering the cuts and bruises that marred her once pristine skin. Without hesitation, she moved to a nearby cabinet, retrieving clean bandages, salves, and other supplies.

"We need to clean her wounds," Alessandra stated, her hands deftly organising the healing implements. Lucien nodded in agreement, concern etched on his face.

Avery's gaze lifted to meet Lucien's, a soft glimmer of thankfulness flickering in her eyes despite her physical exhaustion. In the wake of the turmoil she had faced, his nearness brought a semblance of calm to her frayed nerves. Lucien's eyes conveyed a wealth of unspoken feelings, delivering a wordless pledge of assistance and tenderness despite the trials they had endured together.

Alessandra approached the bedside, her movements graceful and assured. "Brother, help me lift her a bit," she instructed, positioning herself to tend to Avery's wounds.

As they worked together to cleanse and dress

Avery's injuries, a palpable atmosphere of camaraderie and shared purpose filled the room. Lucien's
fingers brushed against Avery's, a silent reassurance
passing between them. Alessandra, despite her no-
nonsense exterior, carried out her healing duties
with a gentle touch that spoke of both skill and
compassion.

The room, bathed in the soft glow of flickering
candles, became a sanctuary of recovery. Outside,
the academy's walls stood as a fortress against the
unknown, proof of resilience to those who called it
home. In the quietude of that moment, they found
solace, knowing that even in the face of darkness,
the bonds forged between them could withstand the
harshest trials.

After the final bandage was delicately secured,
Alessandra gathered her supplies, leaving the room
in respectful silence. Lucien lingered beside Avery,
his eyes reflecting relief and lingering concern.

Tears burst forth from Avery, unchecked and
heavy with the pent-up anguish of her recent ordeal.
Each sob was a release of the physical scars, the
deep-seated pain, and the swirling uncertainty of the
future. Beside her, Lucien's presence was a steady
anchor. He sat close, his arms wrapping around her
in a protective cocoon, his own heart echoing each of

her emotional quakes. His whispers of comfort mingled with her cries, words of solace that sought to soothe the ache within her.

As Avery clung to him, her tears leaving damp trails on his shirt, the room seemed to hold its breath. It absorbed the soft, sorrowful sounds of her weeping, bearing silent witness to the profound impact the events had left on her soul.

Her voice quivered as she spoke. "I... I thought I'd never see you again. When Darmon—"

Softly, Lucien responded, "We don't have to talk about it now. Just know that I'm here, always."

He continued to hold her, a steady anchor in the tempest of her emotions. The love between them was a sanctuary that transcended the horrors they had faced. Lucien's heart ached witnessing Avery's pain, yet he remained resolute in being her steadfast support.

Through her sobs, Avery whispered, "I was so scared, Lucien. I thought I'd lost everything."

"You have lost nothing, Avery. We'll face whatever comes together. You're the love of my life, and nothing will ever change that."

His sincere words carried the weight of a deep commitment. In that vulnerable moment, amid the scars and tears, they discovered a profound connection that no darkness could extinguish. Together, they would heal, rebuild, and forge ahead, bound by a love that had withstood the test of shadows.

Avery's eyes held an otherworldly gleam as she looked at Lucien. The transformation into a demon had left its mark, and uncertainty twinkled in her gaze.

Lucien met her questioning look with a tenacity that transcended the supernatural abyss that separated them. "We'll fix this, Avery. I promise you. You're not alone in this, and I won't rest until we bring you back."

Avery's expression shifted between disbelief and a glimmer of hope. Undoubtedly, the seriousness of her demonic condition was clear, but Lucien's determination kept her steady amidst the sea of uncertainty.

"The manuscript..." Lucien explained, his voice carrying a note of urgency. "It holds secrets that might help us. Ash, with his extensive knowledge of arcane arts, can decipher it. Together, we'll undo what Darmon did to you."

As Lucien spoke, he held her gaze, trying to convey both reassurance and the unyielding commitment to restoring her humanity. The Manual of Demonic Magic, a tome steeped in dark mysteries, became a glimmer of anticipation in the face of despair.

Avery nodded slowly. In that shared moment, a silent vow passed between them—a pledge to defy the demonic chains that bound her and rediscover the light that had once defined her essence.

As Avery succumbed to exhaustion, Lucien gently tucked a strand of hair behind her ear. His gaze held a blend of affection and worry as he observed her serene yet delicate slumber.

Lucien exited the room, each step measured and deliberate, embodying a quiet determination. As he gently closed the door behind him, the muted click resonated softly in the corridor. The academy's halls, which had once reverberated with the ominous presence of the Order, now lay in a respectful hush. With purpose, Lucien navigated the silent passage-ways, making his way to where the rest of the team was gathered.

Entering the dimly lit chamber, he was met with the concerned gazes of his companions. Ash, Jade, Vlad, and Madame Leana formed a tightly knit circle, their expressions mirroring the seriousness of their recent ordeal. They each carried the weight of the recent chaos in their own way, their faces revealing a combination of concern and the weariness that accompanies a hard-fought victory.

Lucien addressed them, his voice a mix of weariness and resolution. "Avery's resting for now. We need to make haste. The Manual of Demonic Magic might be our key to reversing what's been done to her. Ash, your expertise is crucial for deciphering this."

Ash nodded solemnly, understanding the gravity of their quest. "I'll get started right away. This is delicate work, and we can't afford mistakes."

Madame Leana spoke next, her gaze piercing through the shadows. "Time is of the essence. The longer we delay..."

Jade, her eyes reflecting empathy, added, "We're with you, Lucien. Whatever it takes to save Avery."

Vlad, usually the calm voice of reason, chimed in. "Let's not forget the dangers that lie within the Manuscript. It's a path of shadows we tread."

Lucien nodded. "We face the uncertain, but Avery deserves every effort. We won't let her slip away into darkness."

As the group prepared to delve into the mysteries of demonic magic, a collective tenacity replaced the earlier discord. The manuscript awaited, its pages holding the promise of redemption or the hazardous depths of the unknown.

As Ash meticulously deciphered the cryptic passages of the manuscript, an electric tension gripped the chamber. The ancient symbols responded to his expertise, their luminescence pulsating with an otherworldly energy. An atmosphere of anticipation enveloped the surroundings, with every heartbeat resonating the significance of the moment.

Lucien couldn't tear his eyes away from the unfolding magic, a kaleidoscope of colours dancing in the room. The tome seemed alive, its secrets eager to be revealed. It was both a spectacle and a conduit to the unknown.

When the magical tempest subsided, a figure materialised at the heart of the room, enveloped in a wispy cloud of smoke. Slowly taking form, the silhouette transformed into the familiar visage of a man in an antiquated suit—Jarvis de Winter.

Alessandra gasped, her hand instinctively covering her mouth. Lucien remained fixed in place, surprise and happiness dancing across his expression. The others shared glances of incredulity, attempting to grasp the reality of the miraculous scene.

With a hesitant step forward, Lucien's voice trembled with emotion. "Father, is it truly you? How... how can this be?"

Jarvis cast a sombre smile toward his children. "The dark forces inadvertently forged a link between us through the Manuscript. I've witnessed your struggles, your victories. The untiring spirit that has kept you fighting."

Tears glistened in Alessandra's eyes as she approached her father. "We thought we had lost you. Did the tome somehow bring you back to us?"

Jarvis nodded, a hint of sorrow in his gaze. "Yes, my daughter. The Manuscript, originally a tool of darkness, became an unintended vessel for me to communicate with you. But this connection is fragile, and my presence here is fleeting."

Madame Leana's perceptive gaze mirrored the significance of the moment. "What is the path forward, Jarvis? How can we liberate you from this state of limbo?"

Jarvis turned his gaze toward the Manuscript, determination mingled with sadness in his eyes. "To sever the bond, you must perform a ritual outlined in the book. But be cautious, for it is fraught with danger. The forces that ensnared me are not easily trifled with."

His grave expression deepened as he continued to impart crucial information. "When you release me, other entities from the realms beyond may attempt to breach through the opening. It is imperative that you act swiftly. Once I am fully present, destroy the tome to seal the gateway and prevent any malevolent forces from entering."

The room fell into a contemplative hush. The burden of the responsibility they shouldered weighed heavily on every member of the group.

Lucien, his voice steadying, addressed his father. "Father, we've faced formidable challenges, and Avery, the love of my life, is ensnared in a web of darkness. We must save her before we proceed with the ritual. Can the Manuscript guide us to break her transformation into a demon?"

Jarvis nodded, acknowledging the urgency of Lucien's plea. "The Manuscript holds the answers you seek. Use its guidance wisely, for the forces that ensnare Avery are likely entwined with those that bound me."

A renewed sense of purpose swept through the room as Ash and the others focused on deciphering the book's passages related to Avery's predicament. Lucien's thoughts raced, torn between the joy of his father's return and the urgency to rescue Avery.

In the quiet intensity of the chamber, plans took shape. Lucien, Alessandra, and their allies prepared to confront the looming challenges that intertwined their fates with forces beyond the mortal realm. The Manuscript, a key to both salvation and peril, awaited their next move in pursuing light within the shadows.

Lucien's gaze bore into Jarvis, seeking answers within the depths of his father's spectral visage. "Do you know who bound you into that book?"

Jarvis sighed, a haunting echo of breath within the ethereal space surrounding him. "The one who did this to me is a formidable practitioner of dark magic, veiled in shadows. I could never find out their true identity. The cloak of anonymity was their greatest weapon."

Lucien clenched his jaw, frustration coursing through him. The enigmatic nature of his father's captor added another layer of complexity to their treacherous quest. The Manuscript lay open before them, its arcane secrets waiting to be unveiled.

Alessandra, standing beside Lucien, sensed his turmoil. She placed a reassuring hand on his shoulder, silently communicating solidarity and strength. Lucien acknowledged her gesture with a brief, grateful glance before turning back to Jarvis.

"Avery was transformed, not cursed?" Jarvis mused, his spectral form seeming to shimmer with realisation. "I had some suspicions about him back when I was still part of the Order. The darkness that surrounds him is ancient, and his ambitions are boundless."

Lucien took a deep breath as he addressed Jarvis. "There's something you need to know. Lord Darmon is no more. He met his end in the shadows he sought to command."

The silence that followed Lucien's revelation seemed to stretch into eternity. Jarvis, enveloped in the residual magic of the tome, took in the gravity of the news. The room held its breath, waiting for Jarvis to respond to the demise of the malevolent figure who had orchestrated so much suffering.

Finally, Jarvis spoke, his spectral voice carrying a mixture of relief and contemplation. "Darmon's passing marks a significant turn of events. Yet, be wary, for the echoes of his darkness may still reverberate in unforeseen ways."

The gravity of the situation hung in the air, intertwining the destinies of the de Winter family with the malevolent forces seeking dominion. Lucien's mind churned with concern for Avery.

Chapter 13

LUCIEN FELT THE WEIGHT OF RESPONSIBILITY PRESSING on his shoulders as the tome lay open before them, its pages filled with esoteric symbols and cryptic incantations. The room, awash in the gentle flicker of candlelight, appeared to be suspended in a moment of expectant silence.

Vlad, his stoic demeanour betraying a glimmer of confidence, exchanged a knowing glance with Ash. "We've faced difficult challenges before. This will be no different. We'll be fine."

Ash, with a subtle nod, echoed Vlad's assurance. "Dark magic can be unravelled, especially with the right guidance. We've got this."

Jarvis, the ethereal presence hovering beside the open Manuscript, spoke with a spectral calmness. "The spell you seek lies within these pages. Turn to the section marked by the heavenly symbol."

Lucien, his fingers tracing the strange characters, found the designated page. His gaze locked onto the celestial symbol that marked the crucial page and took a steadying breath. The book's ancient pages rustled softly as if whispering secrets that only he could comprehend. The symbols glowed faintly in response to the group's collective intent.

Clearing his throat, Lucien recited the intricate spell, each word carrying the weight of centuries-old magic. The incantation flowed from his lips, a dance of syllables that resonated with the energies swirling around them.

"By the moon's silver light and the sun's golden embrace, we beseech the realms of magic and grace. Shadows that bind, shadows that veil, unravel their hold on this cursed shroud."

The Manuscript responded to his words, the markings on the page shimmering with ghostly luminescence. Alessandra, standing beside him, mirrored his focus, her own power intertwining with his as they cast their combined force into the incantation.

Vlad and Ash, the experts in the dark arts, observed with keen concentration, ensuring the precision of Lucien's recitation. The air became charged with a palpable tension, a symphony of magical currents converging in the small chamber.

Madame Leana, her eyes closed in deep meditation, emanated a spiritual aura that augmented the potency of the spell. Her connection to the ancient forces lent an additional layer of strength to the unfolding ritual.

Lucien continued, his voice resonating with resolve. "By the Earth's steadfast might and the winds that weave through day and night, break the chains that bind this soul, restore the one who's lost control."

As Lucien's voice filled the room, the pages of the book fluttered of their own accord. Each turn revealed new symbols that seemed to dance in time with his words. The air pulsed with the gathering of magical forces, creating a palpable tension as if reality itself was warping in response to their efforts to counteract the dark transformation.

Alessandra, her eyes shimmering with a faint, silvery light, channelled her own magical essence into the chant. The bond between her and Lucien deepened in that shared moment of arcane communion.

At the peak of Lucien's incantation, the celestial symbol in the page's centre glowed with a luminous otherworldly light. The culmination of their efforts hung in the balance, and the fate of Avery rested upon the convoluted dance of words and symbols woven by the group's collective magic.

"In the name of love that transcends the darkest abyss, let the transformation be broken, let the light reminisce. By the power within and the bonds we defend, let Avery's true self ascend."

As the chamber echoed with the last words, the remaining syllable hung in the air like a spell waiting to unfold. The Manuscript's pages returned to stillness. The group waited in silence, expecting the spell's effect on Avery's soul.

The room held its breath as a gentle tremor seemed to pass through the air. It was as if the unseen forces had caught the intangible echo of Lucien's spell and the magical currents resonated with the intent woven into the incantation.

A hushed anticipation lingered. Lucien's heart pounded in rhythm with the shared hope of the group. They stared at the tome, their eyes searching for any sign of change.

Then, a soft glow emanated from the pages of the ancient book, casting a warm light that bathed the chamber. The celestial symbol at the centre of the spell pulsed, its radiance expanding like ripples on a tranquil pond.

Alessandra, her hand still resting on the Manuscript, felt the subtle shift in energy. Her eyes grew wide in awe. "It's working," she murmured, her voice tinged with wonder.

Vlad, ever composed, nodded with a knowing smile. "The magic is taking hold. Now we must wait and trust in its course."

Madame Leana, her spiritual senses attuned to the mystical realms, muttered, "The threads of fate are weaving a new pattern. Let us be patient and steadfast in our vigil."

As the glow intensified, a serene warmth enveloped the group, a reassurance that their consolidated efforts had set in motion forces beyond their immediate comprehension.

Then, in a delicate cascade, the light extended beyond the Manuscript, forming ethereal tendrils that floated towards the centre of the room. The magical threads converged, swirling together in a mesmerising dance.

Amid this arcane ballet, a figure materialised. It was as if the very essence of the chamber had coalesced into a form, slowly taking shape with each passing moment.

A gasp escaped Lucien's lips as the silhouette solidified into a familiar figure. Avery stood before them, bathed in the soft radiance of the magical light. Her eyes, once clouded by demonic influence, now sparkled with recognition and clarity.

A hush fell over the room as the group beheld the wondrous transformation. Avery, freed from the shackles of the demonic curse, looked around with confusion and wonder.

Lucien, his heart overflowing with relief and joy,

took a tentative step forward. "Avery?" he called, his voice a gentle inquiry.

She turned to him. Their eyes met. The connection between them, tested and tempered by the trials of darkness, radiated with an unbreakable strength. Avery's gaze, filled with love and gratitude, spoke volumes that words could not convey.

"You've done it," she said, her voice carrying the echoes of a soul reborn.

As the group basked in the glow of their success, a subtle tremor passed through the spectral form of Jarvis de Winter. His translucent figure wavered, and a hint of weariness etched into his features.

Madame Leana, perceptive to the nuances of the spirit realm, sensed a shift in the force. She stepped forward with concern and asked, "Jarvis, are you all right?"

Jarvis managed a faint smile, but his voice carried both gratitude and farewell. "Releasing me has taken a toll on my soul. The connection to the Manuscript sustained me, but its purpose is fulfilled. I am grateful for this moment of freedom."

Lucien, realising the sacrifice Jarvis had made for Avery's sake, felt a mixture of gratitude and sorrow. "Thank you, Father. You've played a crucial role in saving Avery."

As Jarvis faded, he extended a spectral hand toward Lucien. "Protect her, son. The darkness is not fully vanquished. Be vigilant."

With those parting words, Jarvis dissipated into a soft mist that merged once more with the Manuscript. The room, once again steeped in quiet stillness, held the lingering essence of a soul that had returned to the confines of the enchanted book.

As the ethereal mist of Jarvis de Winter dissolved once more into the tome, Lucien's gaze lingered on the closed book, a deep sense of gratitude and determination welling within him. Turning to the group, he spoke with resolute conviction.

"I promise you all, I will find the spell or any means necessary to release him permanently. His sacrifice won't be in vain. Father deserves the peace he sought for so long."

Avery, now fully restored, looked at Lucien with a profound understanding. "He did save me," she whispered, her eyes reflecting the depth of emotions stirred by the moment.

Lucien nodded, his heart heavy with the weight of the responsibility ahead. "The darkness may linger, but together, we'll face whatever comes our way."

The group, unified by the bonds forged in adversity, stood in silent acknowledgment of the events that had transpired. The Manual of Demonic Magic, now closed, held the secrets of both peril and redemption, the intricate dance between light and shadow that defined their journey.

THE END

WORD FROM THE AUTHOR

Hello, lovelies!

My heart sings with gratitude that you have journeyed with me through the pages of my books. As a writer who spins tales of enchantment and mystery, I am thrilled to offer you a chance to escape reality and enter into the realm of imagination.

As you delve deeper into my books, you will discover a world of infinite possibility, where love, magic, and adventure abound. My stories will transport you to places you've never been before and introduce you to characters that will linger in your heart long after the final page is turned.

My artistry is not complete without your voice. Your reviews are like the wind that carries my stories to new heights and helps me connect with readers like you who cherish the magic of storytelling.

So, if my books have cast a spell on you, bewitched you with their charm, or enchanted you with their tales, please consider leaving a review. Your words are the lantern that guides me on my journey as a writer and helps others find their way to the mystical world we have created together.

Thank you, my lovelies, for the gift of your time and imagination. Let us continue to weave enchanting stories that inspire and delight.

Corinne M Knight

xoxo

ABOUT CORINNE M. KNIGHT

I was born in the mystical land of Romania, a place where legends come alive and magic runs deep. As a child, I was entranced by the stories of the supernatural creatures that roamed the Carpathian Mountains. It was no surprise that I fell in love with writing paranormal romance novels, infusing them with the enchanting magic of my motherland.

While I currently reside in the bustling city of Cardiff with my beloved husband, my heart yearns for the rugged wilderness of Scotland. It's a place that ignites my imagination and inspires me to create stories that transport readers to far-off lands, where love, passion, and the supernatural intertwine.

As a fervent student of history, I find inspiration in exploring the secrets of the past. My dream is to one day live in a grand castle where I can immerse myself in the rich tapestry of historical tales and draw upon them to create new and captivating stories.

To keep up with my latest literary adventures and my upcoming trip to the Scottish Highlands, join my newsletter. And for a chance to win magical give-aways and be the first to hear about my latest book releases, come hang out with me!

ALSO BY CORINNE M. KNIGHT

Of Knights and Monsters series – Paranormal and Urban Fantasy Romance:

The Dark Heir

The King of the Undead

The Demon Prince

The Assassin Heiress

The Veiled Huntress

The Shadowbound Knight

More news regarding the series and the world of the Order of the Dragon will be announced soon. Subscribe to Corinne's <u>newsletter</u> to be the first to know.

Milton Keynes UK
Ingram Content Group UK Ltd.
UKHW041156240324
439902UK00001B/16

9 781914 969102